THE
SARGASSO
OF SPACE

AND TWO OTHERS

THE SARGASSO OF SPACE

AND TWO OTHERS

EDMOND HAMILTON

WILDSIDE PRESS

THE SARGASSO OF SPACE AND TWO OTHERS

"The Sargasso of Space" was originally published in the September, 1931 issue of *Astounding Stories* magazine. "The Man Who Saw the Future" was originally published in the February, 1961 issue of *Amazing Stories*. "The Stars, My Brothers" was originally published in the May, 1962 issue of *Amazing Stories Fact and Science Fiction*.

This edition published in 2009 by Wildside Press, LLC.
www.wildsidepress.com

CONTENTS

THE SARGASSO OF SPACE 7

THE MAN WHO SAW THE FUTURE 32

THE STARS, MY BROTHERS. 46

THE SARGASSO OF SPACE

Captain Crain faced his crew calmly. "We may as well face the facts, men," he said. "The ship's fuel-tanks are empty and we are drifting through space toward the dead-area."

The twenty-odd officers and men gathered on the middle-deck of the freighter *Pallas* made no answer, and Crain continued:

"We left Jupiter with full tanks, more than enough fuel to take us to Neptune. But the leaks in the starboard tanks lost us half our supply, and we had used the other half before discovering that. Since the ship's rocket-tubes cannot operate without fuel, we are simply drifting. We would drift on to Neptune if the attraction of Uranus were not pulling us to the right. That attraction alters our course so that in three ship-days we shall drift into the dead-area."

Rance Kent, first-officer of the *Pallas*, asked a question: "Couldn't we, raise Neptune with the radio, sir, and have them send out a fuel-ship in time to reach us?"

"It's impossible, Mr. Kent," Crain answered. "Our main radio is dead without fuel to run its dynamotors, and our auxiliary set hasn't the power to reach Neptune."

"Why not abandon ship in the space-suits," asked Liggett, the second-officer, "and trust to the chance of some ship picking us up?"

The captain shook his head. "It would be quite useless, for we'd simply drift on through space with the ship into the dead-area."

The score of members of the crew, bronzed space-sailors out of every port in the solar system, had listened mutely. Now, one of them, a tall tube-man, stepped forward a little.

"Just what is this dead-area, sir?" he asked. "I've heard of it, but as this is my first outer-planet voyage, I know nothing about it."

"I'll admit I know little more," said Liggett, "save that a good many disabled ships have drifted into it and have never come out."

"The dead area," Crain told them, "is a region of space ninety thousand miles across within Neptune's orbit, in which the ordinary gravitational attractions of the solar system are dead. This is because in that region the pulls of the sun and the outer planets exactly balance each other. Because of that, anything in the dead-area, will stay in there until time ends, unless it has power of its own. Many wrecked space-ships have drifted into it at one time or another, none ever emerging; and it's believed that there is a great mass of wrecks somewhere in the area, drawn and held together by mutual attraction."

"And we're drifting in to join them," Kent said. "Some prospect!"

"Then there's really no chance for us?" asked Liggett keenly.

Captain Crain thought. "As I see it, very little," he admitted. "If our auxiliary radio can reach some nearby ship before the *Pallas* enters the dead-area, we'll have a chance. But it seems a remote one."

He addressed himself to the men: "I have laid the situation frankly before you because I consider you entitled to the truth. You must remember, however, that while there is life there is hope.

"There will be no change in ship routine, and the customary watches will be kept. Half-rations of food and water will be the rule from now on, though. That is all."

As the men moved silently off, the captain looked after them with something of pride.

"They're taking it like men," he told Kent and Liggett. "It's a pity there's no way out for them and us."

"If the *Pallas* does enter the dead-area and join the wreck-pack," Liggett said, "how long will we be able to live?"

"Probably for some months on our present condensed air and food supplies," Crain answered. "I would prefer, myself, a quicker end."

"So would I," said Kent. "Well, there's nothing left but to pray for some kind of ship to cross our path in the next day or two."

Kent's prayers were not answered in the next ship-day, nor in the next. For, though one of the *Pallas*' radio-operators was constantly at the instruments under Captain Crain's orders, the weak calls of the auxiliary set raised no response.

Had they been on the Venus or Mars run, Kent told himself, there would be some chance, but out here in the vast spaces, between the outer planets, ships were fewer and farther between. The big, cigar-shaped freighter drifted helplessly on in a broad curve toward the dreaded area, the green light-speck of Neptune swinging to their left.

On the third ship-day Kent and Captain Crain stood in the pilot-house behind Liggett, who sat at the now useless rocket-tube controls. Their eyes were on the big glass screen of the gravograph. The black dot on it that represented their ship was crawling steadily toward the bright red circle that stood for the dead-area. . . .

They watched silently until the dot had crawled over the circle's red line, heading toward its center.

"Well, we're in at last," Kent commented. "There seems to be no change in anything, either."

Crain pointed to the instrument-panel. "Look at the gravito-meters."

Kent did. "All dead! No gravitational pull from any direction — no, that one shows a slight attraction from ahead!"

"Then gravitational attraction of some sort does exist in the dead-area after all!" Liggett exclaimed.

"You don't understand," said Crain. "That attraction from ahead is the pull of the wreck-pack at the dead-area's center."

"And it's pulling the *Pallas* toward it?" Kent exclaimed.

Crain nodded. "We'll probably reach the wreck-pack in two more ship-days."

The next two ship-days seemed to Kent drawn out endlessly. A moody silence had grown upon the officers and men of the ship. All seemed oppressed by the strange forces of fate that had seized the ship and were carrying it, smoothly and soundlessly, into this region of irrevocable doom.

The radio-operators' vain calls had ceased. The *Pallas* drifted on into the dreaded area like some dumb ship laden with damned souls. It drifted on, Kent told himself, as many a wrecked and disabled ship had done before it, with the ordinary activities and life of the solar system forever behind it, and mystery and death ahead.

It was toward the end of the second of those two ship-days that Liggett's voice came down from the pilot-house:

"Wreck-pack in sight ahead!"

"We've arrived, anyway!" Kent cried, as he and Crain hastened up into the pilot house. The crew was running to the deck-windows.

"Right ahead there, about fifteen degrees left," Liggett told Kent and Crain, pointing. "Do you see it?"

Kent stared; nodded. The wreck-pack was a distant, disk-like mass against the star-flecked heavens, a mass that glinted here and there in the feeble sunlight of space. It did not seem large, but, as they drifted steadily closer in the next hours, they saw that in reality the wreck-pack was tremendous, measuring at least fifty miles across.

Its huge mass was a heterogeneous heap, composed mostly of countless cigar-like space-ships in all stages of wreckage. Some appeared smashed almost out of all recognizable shape, while others were, to all appearances unharmed. They floated together in this dense mass in space, crowded against one another by their mutual attraction.

There seemed to be among them every type of ship known in the solar system, from small, swift mail-boats to big freighters. And, as they drifted nearer, the three in the pilot-house could see that around and between the ships of the wreck-pack floated much other matter — fragments of wreckage, meteors, small and large, and space-debris of every sort.

The *Pallas* was drifting, not straight toward the wreck-pack, but in a course that promised to take the ship past it.

"We're not heading into the wreck-pack!" Liggett exclaimed. "Maybe we'll drift past it, and on out the dead-area's other side!"

Captain Crain smiled mirthlessly. "You're forgetting your space-mechanics, Liggett. We will drift along the wreck-pack's edge, and then will curve in and go round it in a closing spiral until we reach its edge."

"Lord, who'd have thought there were so many wrecks here!" Kent marvelled. "There must be thousands of them!"

"They've been collecting here ever since the first interplanetary rocket-ships went forth," Crain reminded him. "Not only meteor-wrecked ships, but ships whose mechanisms went wrong — or that ran out of fuel like ours — or that were captured and sacked, and then set adrift by space-pirates."

The *Pallas* by then was drifting along the wreck-pack's rim at a half-mile distance, and Kent's eyes were running over the mass.

"Some of those ships look entirely undamaged. Why couldn't we find one that has fuel in its tanks, transfer it to our own tanks, and get away?" he asked.

Crain's eyes lit. "Kent, that's a real chance! There must be some ships in that pack with fuel in them, and we can use the space-suits to explore for them!"

"Look, we're beginning to curve in around the pack now!" Liggett exclaimed.

The *Pallas*, as though loath to pass the wreck-pack, was curving inward to follow its rim. In the next hours it continued to sail slowly around the great pack, approaching closer and closer to its edge.

In those hours Kent and Crain and all in the ship watched with a fascinated interest that even knowledge of their own peril could not kill. They could see swift-lined passenger-ships of the Pluto and Neptune runs shouldering against small space-yachts with the insignia of Mars or Venus on their bows. Wrecked freighters from Saturn or Earth floated beside rotund grain-boats from Jupiter.

The debris among the pack's wrecks was just as varied, holding fragments of metal, dark meteors of differing size — and many human bodies. Among these were some clad in the insulated space-suits, with their transparent glassite helmets. Kent wondered what wreck they had abandoned hastily in those suits, only to be swept with it into the dead-area, to die in their suits.

By the end of that ship-day, the *Pallas*, having floated almost completely around the wreck-pack, finally struck the wrecks at its edge with a jarring shock; then bobbed for a while and lay still. From pilot-house and deck windows the men looked eagerly forth.

Their ship floated at the wreck-pack's edge. Directly to its right floated a sleek, shining Uranus-Jupiter passenger-ship whose bows had been smashed in by a meteor. On their left bobbed an unmarked freighter of the old type with projecting rocket-tubes, apparently intact. Beyond them in the wreck-pack lay another Uranus craft, a freighter, and, beyond it, stretched the countless other wrecks.

Captain Crain summoned the crew together again on the middle-deck.

"Men, we've reached the wreck-pack at the dead-area's center, and here we'll stay until the end of time unless we get out under our own power. Mr. Kent has suggested a possible way of doing so, which I consider highly feasible.

"He has suggested that in some of the ships in the wreck-pack may be found enough fuel to enable us to escape from the dead-area, once it is transferred to this ship. I am going to permit him to explore the wreck-pack with a party in space suits, and I am asking for volunteers for this service."

The entire crew stepped quickly forward. Crain smiled.

"Twelve of you will be enough," he told them. "The eight tube-men and four of the cargo-men will go, therefore, with Mr. Kent and Mr. Liggett as leaders. Mr. Kent, you may address the men if you wish."

"Get down to the lower airlock and into your space-suits at once, then," Kent told them. "Mr. Liggett, will you supervise that?"

As Liggett and the men trooped down to the airlock, Kent turned back toward his superior.

"There's a very real chance of your becoming lost in this huge wreck-pack, Kent," Crain told him: "so be very careful to keep your bearings at all times. I know I can depend on you."

"I'll do my best," Kent was saying, when Liggett's excited face reappeared suddenly at the stair.

"There are men coming toward the *Pallas* along the wreck-pack's edge!" he reported — "a half-dozen men in space-suits!"

"You must be mistaken, Liggett!" exclaimed Crain. "They must be some of the bodies in space-suits we saw in the pack."

"No, they're living men!" Liggett cried. "They're coming straight toward us — come down and see!"

Crain and Kent followed Liggett quickly down to the airlock room, where the men who had started donning their space-suits were now peering excitedly from the windows. Crain and Kent looked where Liggett pointed, along the wreck-pack's edge to the ship's right.

Six floating shapes, men in space-suits, were approaching along the pack's border. They floated smoothly through space, reaching the wrecked passenger-ship beside the *Pallas*. They braced their feet against its side and propelled themselves on through the void like swimmers under water, toward the *Pallas*.

"They must be survivors from some wreck that drifted in here as we did!" Kent exclaimed. "Maybe they've lived here for months!"

"It's evident that they saw the *Pallas* drift into the pack, and have come to investigate," Crain estimated. "Open the airlock for them, men, for they'll want to come inside."

Two of the men spun the wheels that slid aside the airlock's outer door. In a moment the half-dozen men outside had reached the ship's side, and had pulled themselves down inside the airlock.

When all were in, the outer door was closed, and air hissed in to fill the lock. The airlock's inner door then slid open and the newcomers stepped into the ship's interior, unscrewing their transparent helmets as they did so. For a few moments the visitors silently surveyed their new surroundings.

Their leader was a swarthy individual with sardonic black eyes who, on noticing Crain's captain-insignia, came toward him with outstretched hand. His followers seemed to be cargo-men or deck-men, looking hardly intelligent enough to Kent's eyes to be tube-men.

"Welcome to our city!" their leader exclaimed as he shook Crain's hand. "We saw your ship drift in, but hardly expected to find anyone living in it."

"I'll confess that we're surprised ourselves to find any life here," Crain told him. "You're living on one of the wrecks?"

The other nodded. "Yes, on the *Martian Queen*, a quarter-mile along the pack's edge. It was a Saturn-Neptune passenger ship, and about a month ago we were at this cursed dead-area's edge, when half our rocket-tubes exploded. Eighteen of us escaped the explosion, the ship's walls still being tight; and we drifted into the pack here, and have been living here ever since."

"My name's Krell," he added, "and I was a tube-man on the ship. I and another of the tube-men, named Jandron, were the highest in rank left, all the officers and other tube-men having been killed, so we took charge and have been keeping order."

"What about your passengers?" Liggett asked.

"All killed but one," Krell answered. "When the tubes let go they smashed up the whole lower two decks."

Crain briefly explained to him the *Pallas'* predicament. "Mr. Kent and Mr. Liggett were on the point of starting a search of the wreck-pack for fuel when you arrived," he said, "With enough fuel we can get clear of the dead-area."

Krell's eyes lit up. "That would mean a getaway for all of us! It surely ought to be possible!"

"Do you know whether there are any ships in the pack with fuel in their tanks?" Kent asked. Krell shook his head.

"We've searched through the wreck-pack a good bit, but never bothered about fuel, it being no good to us. But there ought to be some, at least: there's enough wrecks in this cursed place to make it possible to find almost anything.

"You'd better not start exploring, though," he added, "without some of us along as guides, for I'm here to tell you that you can lose yourself in this wreck-pack without knowing it. If you wait until to-morrow, I'll come over myself and go with you."

"I think that would be wise," Crain said to Kent. "There is plenty of time."

"Time is the one thing there's plenty of in this damned place," Krell agreed. "We'll be getting back to the *Martian Queen* now and give the good news to Jandron and the rest."

"Wouldn't mind if Liggett and I came along, would you?" Kent asked. "I'd like to see how your ship's fixed — that is, if it's all right with you, sir," he added to his superior.

Crain nodded. "All right if you don't stay long," he said. But, to Kent's surprise Krell seemed reluctant to endorse his proposal.

"I guess it'll be all right," he said slowly, "though there's nothing much on the *Martian Queen* to see."

Krell and his followers replaced their helmets and returned into the airlock. Liggett followed them, and, as Kent struggled hastily into a space-suit, he found Captain Crain at his side.

"Kent, look sharp when you get over on that ship," Crain told him. "I don't like the look of this Krell, and his story about all the officers being killed in the explosion sounds fishy to me."

"To me, too," Kent agreed. "But Liggett and I will have the suit-phones in our space-suits and can call you from there in case of need."

Crain nodded, and Kent with space-suit on and transparent helmet screwed tight, stepped into the airlock with the rest. The airlock's inner door closed, the outer one opened, and as the air puffed out into space, Kent and Krell and Liggett leapt out into the void, the others following.

It was no novelty to Kent to float in a space-suit in the empty void. He and the others now floated as smoothly as though under water toward a wrecked liner at the *Pallas'* right. They reached it, pulled themselves around it, and, with feet braced against its side, propelled themselves on through space along the border of the wreck-pack.

They passed a half-dozen wrecks thus, before coming to the *Martian Queen*. It was a silvery, glistening ship whose stern and lower walls were bulging and strained, but not cracked. Kent told himself that Krell had spoken truth about the exploding rocket-tubes, at least.

They struck the *Martian Queen's* side and entered the upper-airlock open for them. Once through the airlock they found themselves on the ship's upper-deck. And when Kent and Liggett removed their helmets with the others they found a full dozen men confronting them, a brutal-faced group who exhibited some surprise at sight of them.

Foremost among them stood a tall, heavy individual who regarded Kent and Liggett with the cold, suspicious eyes of an animal.

"My comrade and fellow-ruler here, Wald Jandron," said Krell. To Jandron he explained rapidly. "The whole crew of the *Pallas* is alive, and they say if they can find fuel in the wreck-pack their ship can get out of here."

"Good," grunted Jandron. "The sooner they can do it, the better it will be for us."

Kent saw Liggett flush angrily, but he ignored Jandron and spoke to Krell. "You said one of your passengers had escaped the explosion?"

To Kent's amazement a girl stepped from behind the group of men, a slim girl with pale face and steady, dark eyes. "I'm the passenger," she told him. "My name's Marta Mallen."

Kent and Liggett stared, astounded. "Good Lord!" Kent exclaimed. "A girl like you on this ship!"

"Miss Mallen happened to be on the upper-deck at the time of the explosion and, so, escaped when the other passengers were killed," Krell explained smoothly. "Isn't that so, Miss Mallen?"

The girl's eyes had not left Kent's, but at Krell's words she nodded. "Yes, that is so," she said mechanically.

Kent collected his whirling thoughts. "But wouldn't you rather go back to the *Pallas* with us?" he asked. "I'm sure you'd be more comfortable there."

"She doesn't go," grunted Jandron. Kent turned in quick wrath toward him, but Krell intervened.

"Jandron only means that Miss Mallen is much more comfortable on this passenger-ship than she'd be in your freighter." He shot a glance at the girl as he spoke, and Kent saw her wince.

"I'm afraid that's so," she said; "but I thank you for the offer, Mr. Kent."

Kent could have sworn that there was an appeal in her eyes, and he stood for a moment, indecisive, Jandron's stare upon him. After a moment's thought he turned to Krell.

"You were going to show me the damage the exploding tubes did," he said, and Krell nodded quickly.

"Of course; you can see from the head of the stair back in the after-deck."

He led the way along a corridor, Jandron and the girl and two of the men coming with them. Kent's thoughts were still chaotic as he walked between Krell and Liggett. What was this girl doing amid the men of the *Martian Queen*? What had her eyes tried to tell him?

Liggett nudged his side in the dim corridor, and Kent, looking down, saw dark splotches on its metal floor. Blood-stains! His suspicions strengthened. They might be from the bleeding of those wounded in the tube-explosions. But were they?

They reached the after-deck whose stair's head gave a view of the wrecked tube-rooms beneath. The lower decks had been smashed by terrific forces. Kent's practiced eyes ran rapidly over the shattered rocket-tubes.

"They've back-blasted from being fired too fast," he said. "Who was controlling the ship when this happened?"

"Galling, our second-officer," answered Krell. "He had found us routed too close to the dead-area's edge and was trying to get away from it in a hurry, when he used the tubes too fast, and half of them back-blasted."

"If Galling was at the controls in the pilot-house, how did the explosion kill him?" asked Liggett skeptically. Krell turned quickly.

"The shock threw him against the pilot-house wall and fractured his skull — he died in an hour," he said. Liggett was silent.

"Well, this ship will never move again," Kent said. "It's too bad that the explosion blew out your tanks, but we ought to find fuel somewhere in the wreck-pack for the *Pallas*. And now we'd best get back."

As they returned up the dim corridor Kent managed to walk beside Marta Mallen, and, without being seen, he contrived to detach his suit-phone — the compact little radiophone case inside his space-suit's neck — and slip it into the girl's grasp. He dared utter no word of explanation, but apparently she understood, for she had concealed the suit-phone by the time they reached the upper-deck.

Kent and Liggett prepared to don their space-helmets, and before entering the airlock, Kent turned to Krell.

"We'll expect you at the *Pallas* first hour to-morrow, and we'll start searching the wreck-pack with a dozen of our men," he said.

He then extended his hand to the girl. "Good-by, Miss Mallen. I hope we can have a talk soon."

He had said the words with double meaning, and saw understanding in her eyes. "I hope we can, too," she said.

Kent's nod to Jandron went unanswered, and he and Liggett adjusted their helmets and entered the airlock.

Once out of it, they kicked rapidly away from the *Martian Queen*, floating along with the wreck-pack's huge mass to their right, and only the star-flecked emptiness of infinity to their left. In a few minutes they reached the airlock of the *Pallas*.

They found Captain Crain awaiting them anxiously. Briefly Kent reported everything.

"I'm certain there has been foul play aboard the *Martian*

Queen," he said. "Krell you saw for yourself, Jandron is pure brute, and their men seem capable of anything.

"I gave the suit-phone to the girl, however, and if she can call us with it, we can get the truth from her. She dared not tell me anything there in the presence of Krell and Jandron."

Crain nodded, his face grave. "We'll see whether or not she calls," he said.

Kent took a suit-phone from one of their space-suits and rapidly, tuned it to match the one he had left with Marta Mallen. Almost at once they heard her voice from it, and Kent answered rapidly.

"I'm so glad I got you!" she exclaimed. "Mr. Kent, I dared not tell you the truth about this ship when you were here, or Krell and the rest would have killed you at once."

"I thought that was it, and that's why I left the suit-phone for you," Kent said. "Just what is the truth?"

"Krell and Jandron and these men of theirs are the ones who killed the officers and passengers of the *Martian Queen*! What they told you about the explosion was true enough, for the explosion did happen that way, and because of it, the ship drifted into the dead-area. But the only ones killed by it were some of the tube-men and three passengers.

"Then, while the ship was drifting into the dead-area, Krell told the men that the fewer aboard, the longer they could live on the ship's food and air. Krell and Jandron led the men in a surprise attack and killed all the officers and passengers, and threw their bodies out into space. I was the only passenger they spared, because both Krell and Jandron — want me!"

There was a silence, and Kent felt a red anger rising in him. "Have they dared harm you?" he asked after a moment.

"No, for Krell and Jandron are too jealous of each other to permit the other to touch me. But it's been terrible living with them in this awful place."

"Ask her if she knows what their plans are in regard to us," Crain told Kent.

Marta had apparently overheard the question. "I don't know that, for they shut me in my cabin as soon as you left," she said. "I've heard them talking and arguing excitedly, though. I know that if you do find fuel, they'll try to kill you all and escape from here in your ship."

"Pleasant prospect," Kent commented. "Do you think they plan an attack on us now?"

"No; I think that they'll wait until you've refueled your ship, if you are able to do that, and then try treachery."

"Well, they'll find us ready. Miss Mallen, you have the suit-phone: keep it hidden in your cabin and I'll call you first thing to-morrow. We're going to get you out of there, but we don't want to break with Krell until we're ready. Will you be all right until then?"

"Of course I will," she answered. "There's another thing, though. My name isn't Miss Mallen — it's Marta."

"Mine's Rance," said Kent, smiling. "Good-by until to-morrow, then, Marta."

"Good-by, Rance."

Kent rose from the instrument with the smile still in his eyes, but with his lips compressed. "Damn it, there's the bravest and finest girl in the solar system!" he exclaimed. "Over there with those brutes!"

"We'll have her out, never fear," Crain reassured him. "The main thing is to determine our course toward Krell and Jandron."

Kent thought. "As I see it, Krell can help us immeasurably in our search through the wreck-pack for fuel," he said. "I think it would be best to keep on good terms with him until we've found fuel and have it in our tanks. Then we can turn the tables on them before they can do anything."

Crain nodded thoughtfully. "I think you're right. Then you and Liggett and Krell can head our search-party to-morrow."

Crain established watches on a new schedule, and Kent and Liggett and the dozen men chosen for the exploring party of the next day ate a scanty meal and turned in for some sleep.

When Kent woke and glimpsed the massed wrecks through the window he was for the moment amazed, but rapidly remembered. He and Liggett were finishing their morning ration when Crain pointed to a window.

"There comes Krell now," he said, indicating the single space-suited figure approaching along the wreck-pack's edge.

"I'll call Marta before he gets here," said Kent hastily.

The girl answered on the suit-phone immediately, and it occurred to Kent that she must have spent the night without sleeping. "Krell left a few minutes ago," she said.

"Yes, he's coming now. You heard nothing of their plans?"

"No; they've kept me shut in my cabin. However, I did hear Krell giving Jandron and the rest directions. I'm sure they're plotting something."

"We're prepared for them," Kent assured her. "If all goes well, before you realize it, you'll be sailing out of here with us in the *Pallas*."

"I hope so," she said. "Rance, be careful with Krell in the wreck-pack. He's dangerous."

"I'll be watching him," he promised. "Good-by, Marta."

Kent reached the lower-deck just as Krell entered from the airlock, his swarthy face smiling as he removed his helmet. He carried a pointed steel bar. Liggett and the others were donning their suits.

"All ready to go, Kent?" Krell asked.

Kent nodded. "All ready," he said shortly. Since hearing Marta's story he found it hard to dissimulate with Krell.

"You'll want bars like mine," Krell continued, "for they're damned handy when you get jammed between wreckage masses. Exploring this wreck-pack is no soft job: I can tell you from experience."

Liggett and the rest had their suits adjusted, and with bars in their grasp, followed Krell into the airlock. Kent hung back for a last word with Crain, who, with his half-dozen remaining men, was watching.

"Marta just told me that Krell and Jandron have been plotting something," he told the captain; "so I'd keep a close watch outside."

"Don't worry, Kent. We'll let no one inside the *Pallas* until you and Liggett and the men get back."

In a few minutes they were out of the ship, with Krell and Kent and Liggett leading, and the twelve members of the *Pallas'* crew following closely.

The three leaders climbed up on the Uranus-Jupiter

passenger-ship that lay beside the *Pallas*, the others moving on and exploring the neighboring wrecks in parties of two and three. From the top of the passenger-ship, when they gained it, Kent and his two companions could look far out over the wreck-pack. It was an extraordinary spectacle, this stupendous mass of dead ships floating motionless in the depths of space, with the burning stars above and below them.

His companions and the other men clambering over the neighboring wrecks seemed weird figures in their bulky suits and transparent helmets. Kent looked back at the *Pallas*, and then along the wreck-pack's edge to where he could glimpse the silvery side of the *Martian Queen*. But now Krell and Liggett were descending into the ship's interior through the great opening smashed in its bows, and Kent followed.

They found themselves in the liner's upper navigation-rooms. Officers and men lay about, frozen to death at the instant the meteor-struck vessel's air had rushed out, and the cold of space had entered. Krell led the way on, down into the ship's lower decks, where they found the bodies of the crew and passengers lying in the same silent death.

The salons held beautifully-dressed women, distinguished-looking men, lying about as the meteor's shock had hurled them. One group lay around a card-table, their game interrupted. A woman still held a small child, both seemingly asleep. Kent tried to shake off the oppression he felt as he and Krell and Liggett continued down to the tank-rooms.

They found their quest there useless, for the tanks had been strained by the meteor's shock, and were empty. Kent felt Liggett grasp his hand and heard him speak, the sound-vibrations coming through their contacting suits.

"Nothing here; and we'll find it much the same through all these wrecks, if I'm not wrong. Tanks always give at a shock."

"There must be some ships with fuel still in them among all these," Kent answered.

They climbed back, up to the ship's top, and leapt off it toward a Jupiter freighter lying a little farther inside the pack. As they floated toward it, Kent saw their men moving on with them from ship to ship, progressing inward into the pack. Both Kent and Liggett kept Krell always ahead of them, knowing that a blow from his bar, shattering their glassite helmets, meant instant death. But Krell seemed quite intent on the search for fuel.

The big Jupiter freighter seemed intact from above, but, when they penetrated into it, they found its whole under-side blown away, apparently by an explosion of its tanks. They moved on to the next ship, a private space-yacht, small in size, but luxurious in fittings. It had been abandoned in space, its rocket-tubes burst and tanks strained.

They went on, working deeper into the wreck-pack. Kent almost forgot the paramount importance of their search in the fascination of it. They explored almost every known type of ship — freighters, liners, cold-storage boats, and grain-boats. Once Kent's hopes ran high at sight of a fuel-ship, but it proved to be in ballast, its cargo-tanks empty and its own tanks and tubes apparently blown simultaneously.

Kent's muscles ached from the arduous work of climbing over and exploring the wrecks. He and Liggett had become accustomed to the sight of frozen, motionless bodies.

As they worked deeper into the pack, they noticed that the ships were of increasingly older types, and at last Krell signalled a halt. "We're almost a mile in," he told them, gripping their hands. "We'd better work back out, taking a different section of the pack as we do."

Kent nodded. "It may change our luck," he said.

It did; for when they had gone not more than a half-mile back, they glimpsed one of their men waving excitedly from the top of a Pluto liner.

They hastened at once toward him, the other men gathering also; and when Kent grasped the man's hand he heard his excited voice.

"Fuel-tanks here are more than half-full, sir!"

They descended quickly into the liner, finding that though its whole stern had been sheared away by a meteor, its tanks had remained miraculously unstrained.

"Enough fuel here to take the *Pallas* to Neptune!" Kent exclaimed.

"How will you get it over to your ship?" Krell asked.

Kent pointed to great reels of flexible metal tubing hanging near the tanks.

"We'll pump it over. The *Pallas* has tubing like this ship's, for taking on fuel in space, and, by joining its tubing to this, we'll have a tube-line between the two ships. It's hardly more than a quarter-mile."

"Let's get back and let them know about it," Liggett urged, and they climbed back out of the liner.

They worked their way out of the wreck-pack with much greater speed than that with which they had entered, needing only an occasional brace against a ship's side to send them floating over the wrecks. They came to the wreck-pack's edge at a little distance from the *Pallas*, and hastened toward it.

They found the outer door of the *Pallas'* airlock open, and entered, Krell remaining with them. As the outer door closed and air hissed into the lock, Kent and the rest removed their helmets. The inner door slid open as they were doing this, and from inside almost a score of men leapt upon them!

Kent, stunned for a moment, saw Jandron among their attackers, bellowing orders to them, and even as he struck out furiously he comprehended. Jandron and the men of the *Martian Queen* had somehow captured the *Pallas* from Crain and had been awaiting their return!

The struggle was almost instantly over, for, outnumbered and hampered as they were by their heavy space-suits, Kent and Liggett and their followers had no chance. Their hands, still in the suits, were bound quickly behind them at Jandron's orders.

Kent heard an exclamation, and saw Marta starting toward him from behind Jandron's men. But a sweep of Jandron's arm brushed her rudely back. Kent strained madly at his bonds. Krell's face had a triumphant look.

"Did it all work as I told you it would, Jandron?" he asked.

"It worked," Jandron answered impassively. "When they saw fifteen of us coming from the wreck-pack in space-suits, they opened right up to us."

Kent understood, and cursed Krell's cunning. Crain, seeing the fifteen figures approaching from the wreck-pack, had naturally thought they were Kent's party, and had let them enter to overwhelm his half-dozen men.

"We put Crain and his men over in the *Martian Queen*," Jandron continued, "and took all their helmets so they can't escape. The girl we brought over here. Did you find a wreck with fuel?"

Krell nodded. "A Pluto liner a quarter-mile back, and we

can pump the fuel over here by connecting tube-lines. What the devil —"

Jandron had made a signal at which three of his men had leapt forward on Krell, securing his hands like those of the others.

"Have you gone crazy, Jandron?" cried Krell, his face red with anger and surprise.

"No," Jandron replied impassively; "but the men are as tired as I am of your bossing ways, and have chosen me as their sole leader."

"You dirty double-crosser!" Krell raged. "Are you men going to let him get away with this?"

The men paid no attention, and Jandron motioned to the airlock. "Take them over to the *Martian Queen* too," he ordered, "and make sure there's no space-helmet left there. Then get back at once, for we've got to get the fuel into this ship and make a getaway."

The helmets of Kent and Krell and the other helpless prisoners were put upon them, and, with hands still bound, they were herded into the airlock by eight of Jandron's men attired in space-suits also. The prisoners were then joined one to another by a strand of metal cable.

Kent, glancing back into the ship as the airlock's inner door closed, saw Jandron giving rapid orders to his followers, and noticed Marta held back from the airlock by one of them. Krell's eyes glittered venomously through his helmet. The outer door opened, and their guards jerked them forth into space by the connecting cable.

They were towed helplessly along the wreck-pack's rim toward the *Martian Queen*. Once inside its airlock, Jandron's men removed the prisoners' space-helmets and then used the duplicate-control inside the airlock itself to open the inner door. Through this opening they thrust the captives, those inside the ship not daring to enter the airlock. Jandron's men then closed the inner door, re-opened the outer one, and started back toward the *Pallas* with the helmets of Kent and his companions.

Kent and the others soon found Crain and his half-dozen men who rapidly undid their bonds. Crain's men still wore their space-suits, but, like Kent's companions, were without space-helmets.

"Kent, I was afraid they'd get you and your men too!" Crain exclaimed. "It's all my fault, for when I saw Jandron and his men coming from the wreck-pack I never doubted but that it was you."

"It's no one's fault," Kent told him. "It's just something that we couldn't foresee."

Crain's eyes fell on Krell. "But what's he doing here?" he exclaimed. Kent briefly explained Jandron's treachery toward Krell, and Crain's brows drew ominously together.

"So Jandron put you here with us! Krell, I am a commissioned captain of a space-ship, and as such can legally try you and sentence you to death here without further formalities."

Krell did not answer, but Kent intervened. "There's hardly time for that now, sir," he said. "I'm as anxious to settle with Krell as anyone, but right now our main enemy is Jandron, and Krell hates Jandron worse than we do, if I'm not mistaken."

"You're not," said Krell grimly. "All I want right now is to get within reach of Jandron."

"There's small chance of any of us doing that," Crain told them. "There's not a single space-helmet on the *Martian Queen*."

"You've searched?" Liggett asked.

"Every cubic inch of the ship," Crain told him. "No, Jandron's men made sure there were no helmets left here, and without helmets this ship is an inescapable prison."

"Damn it, there must be some way out!" Kent exclaimed. "Why, Jandron and his men must be starting to pump that fuel into the *Pallas* by now! They'll be sailing off as soon as they do it!"

Crain's face was sad. "I'm afraid this is the end, Kent. Without helmets, the space between the *Martian Queen* and the *Pallas* is a greater barrier to us than a mile-thick wall of steel. In this ship we'll stay, until the air and food give out, and death releases us."

"Damn it, I'm not thinking of myself!" Kent cried. "I'm thinking of Marta! The *Pallas* will sail out of here with her in Jandron's power!"

"The girl!" Liggett exclaimed. "If she could bring us over

space-helmets from the *Pallas* we could get out of here!"

Kent was thoughtful. "If we could talk to her — she must still have that suit-phone I gave her. Where's another?"

Crain quickly detached the compact suit-phone from inside the neck of his own space-suit, and Kent rapidly tuned it to the one he had given Marta Mallen. His heart leapt as her voice came instantly from it:

"Rance! Rance Kent —"

"Marta — this is Rance!" he cried.

He heard a sob of relief. "I've been calling you for minutes! I was hoping that you'd remember to listen!

"Jandron and ten of the others have gone to that wreck in which you found the fuel," she added swiftly. "They unreeled a tube-line behind them as they went, and I can hear them pumping in the fuel now."

"Are the others guarding you?" Kent asked quickly.

"They're down in the lower deck at the tanks and airlocks. They won't allow me down on that deck. I'm up here in the middle-deck, absolutely alone.

"Jandron told me that we'd start out of here as soon as the fuel was in," she added, "and he and the men were laughing about Krell."

"Marta, could you in any way get space-helmets and get out to bring them over here to us?" Kent asked eagerly.

"There's a lot of space-suits and helmets here," she answered, "but I couldn't get out with them, Rance! I couldn't get to the airlocks with Jandron's seven or eight men down there guarding them!"

Kent felt despair; then as an idea suddenly flamed in him, he almost shouted into the instrument:

"Marta, unless you can get over here with helmets for us, we're all lost. I want you to put on a space-suit and helmet at once!"

There was a short silence, and then her voice came, a little muffled. "I've got the suit and helmet on, Rance. I'm wearing the suit-phone inside it."

"Good! Now, can you get up to the pilot-house? There's no

one guarding it or the upper-deck? Hurry up there, then, at once."

Crain and the rest were staring at Kent. "Kent, what are you going to have her do?" Crain exclaimed. "It'll do no good for her to start the *Pallas*: those guards will be up there in a minute!"

"I'm not going to have her start the *Pallas*," said Kent grimly. "Marta, you're in the pilot-house? Do you see the heavy little steel door in the wall beside the instrument-panel?"

"I'm at it, but it's locked with a combination-lock," she said.

"The combination is 6–34–77–81," Kent told her swiftly. "Open it as quickly as you can."

"Good God, Kent!" cried Crain. "You're going to have her — ?"

"Get out of there the only way she can!" Kent finished fiercely. "You have the door open, Marta?"

"Yes; there are six or seven control-wheels inside."

"Those wheels control the *Pallas*' exhaust-valves," Kent told her. "Each wheel opens the valves of one of the ship's decks or compartments and allows its air to escape into space. They're used for testing leaks in the different deck and compartment divisions. Marta, you must turn all those wheels as far as you can to the right."

"But all the ship's air will rush out; the guards below have no suits on, and they'll be —" she was exclaiming. Kent interrupted.

"It's the only chance for you, for all of us. Turn them!"

There was a moment of silence, and Kent was going to repeat the order when her voice came, lower in tone, a little strange:

"I understand, Rance. I'm going to turn them."

There was silence again, and Kent and the men grouped round him were tense. All were envisioning the same thing — the air rushing out of the *Pallas*' valves, and the unsuspecting guards in its lower deck smitten suddenly by an instantaneous death.

Then Marta's voice, almost a sob: "I turned them, Rance. The air puffed out all around me."

"Your space-suit is working all right?"

"Perfectly," she said.

"Then go down and tie together as many space-helmets as you can manage, get out of the airlock, and try to get over here to the *Martian Queen* with them. Do you think you can do that, Marta?"

"I'm going to try," she said steadily. "But I'll have to pass those men in the lower-deck I just — killed. Don't be anxious if I don't talk for a little."

Yet her voice came again almost immediately. "Rance, the pumping has stopped! They must have pumped all the fuel into the *Pallas*!"

"Then Jandron and the rest will be coming back to the *Pallas* at once!" Kent cried. "Hurry, Marta!"

The suit-phone was silent; and Kent and the rest, their faces closely pressed against the deck-windows, peered intently along the wreck-pack's edge. The *Pallas* was hidden from their view by the wrecks between, and there was no sign as yet of the girl.

Kent felt his heart beating rapidly. Crain and Liggett pressed beside him, the men around them; Krell's face was a mask as he too gazed. Kent was rapidly becoming convinced that some mis-chance had overtaken the girl when an exclamation came from Liggett. He pointed excitedly.

She was in sight, unrecognizable in space-suit and helmet, floating along the wreck-pack's edge toward them. A mass of the glassite space-helmets tied together was in her grasp. She climbed bravely over the stern of a projecting wreck and shot on toward the *Martian Queen*.

The airlock's door was open for her, and, when she was inside it, the outer door closed and air hissed into the lock. In a moment she was in among them, still clinging to the helmets. Kent grasped her swaying figure and removed her helmet.

"Marta, you're all right?" he cried.

She nodded a little weakly.

"I'm all right. It was just that I had to go over those guards that were all frozen. . . . Terrible!"

"Get these helmets on!" Crain was crying. "There's a dozen of them, and twelve of us can stop Jandron's men if we get back in time!"

Kent and Liggett and the nearer of their men were swiftly donning the helmets. Krell grasped one and Crain sought to snatch it.

"Let that go! We'll not have you with us when we haven't enough helmets for our own men!"

"You'll have me or kill me here!" Krell cried, his eyes hate-mad. "I've got my own account to settle with Jandron!"

"Let him have it!" Liggett cried. "We've no time now to argue!"

Kent reached toward the girl. "Marta, give one of the men your helmet," he ordered; but she shook her head.

"I'm going with you!" Before Kent could dispute she had the helmet on again, and Crain was pushing them into the air-lock. The nine or ten left inside without helmets hastily thrust steel bars into the men's hands before the inner door closed. The outer one opened and they leapt forth into space, floating smoothly along the wreck-pack's border with bars in their grasp, thirteen strong.

Kent found the slowness with which they floated forward torturing. He glimpsed Crain and Liggett ahead, Marta beside him, Krell floating behind him to the left. They reached the projecting freighters, climbed over and around them, braced against them and shot on. They sighted the *Pallas* ahead now. Suddenly they discerned another group of eleven figures in space-suits approaching it from the wreck-pack's interior, rolling up the tube-line that led from the *Pallas* as they did so. Jandron's party!

Jandron and his men had seen them and were suddenly making greater efforts to reach the *Pallas*. Kent and his companions, propelling themselves frenziedly on from another wreck, reached the ship's side at the same time as Jandron's men. The two groups mixed and mingled, twisted and turned in a mad space-combat.

Kent had been grasped by one of Jandron's men and raised his bar to crack the other's glassite helmet. His opponent caught the bar, and they struggled, twisting and turning over and over far up in space amid a half-score similar struggles. Kent wrenched his bar free at last from the other's grasp and brought it down on his helmet. The glassite cracked, and he caught a glimpse of the man's hate-distorted face frozen instantly in death.

Kent released him and propelled himself toward a struggling trio nearby. As he floated toward them, he saw Jandron beyond them making wild gestures of command and saw Krell approaching Jandron with upraised bar. Kent, on reaching the three combatants, found them to be two of Jandron's men overcoming Crain. He shattered one's helmet as he reached them, but saw the other's bar go up for a blow.

Kent twisted frantically, uselessly, to escape it, but before the blow could descend a bar shattered his opponent's helmet from behind. As the man froze in instant death Kent saw that it was Marta who had struck him from behind. He jerked her to his side. The struggles in space around them seemed to be ending.

Six of Jandron's party had been slain, and three of Kent's companions. Jandron's four other followers were giving up the combat, floating off into the wreck-pack in clumsy, hasty flight. Someone grasped Kent's arm, and he turned to find it was Liggett.

"They're beaten!" Liggett's voice came to him! "They're all killed but those four!"

"What about Jandron himself?" Kent cried. Liggett pointed to two space-suited bodies twisting together in space, with bars still in their lifeless grasp.

Kent saw through their shattered helmets the stiffened faces of Jandron and Krell, their helmets having apparently been broken by each other's simultaneous blows.

Crain had gripped Kent's arm also. "Kent, it's over!" he was exclaiming. "Liggett and I will close the *Pallas'* exhaust-valves and release new air in it. You take over helmets for the rest of our men in the *Martian Queen*."

In several minutes Kent was back with the men from the *Martian Queen*. The *Pallas* was ready, with Liggett in its pilot-house, the men taking their stations, and Crain and Marta awaiting Kent.

"We've enough fuel to take us out of the dead-area and to Neptune without trouble!" Crain declared. "But what about those four of Jandron's men that got away?"

"The best we can do is leave them here," Kent told him. "Best for them, too, for at Neptune they'd be executed, while they can live indefinitely in the wreck-pack."

"I've seen so many men killed on the *Martian Queen* and here," pleaded Marta. "Please don't take them to Neptune."

"All right, we'll leave them," Crain agreed, "though the scoundrels ought to meet justice." He hastened up to the pilot-house after Liggett.

In a moment came the familiar blast of the rocket-tubes, and the *Pallas* shot out cleanly from the wreck-pack's edge. A scattered cheer came from the crew. With gathering speed the ship arrowed out, its rocket-tubes blasting now in steady succession.

Kent, with his arm across Marta's shoulders, watched the wreck-pack grow smaller behind. It lay as when he first had seen it, a strange great mass, floating forever motionless among the brilliant stars. He felt the girl beside him shiver, and swung her quickly around.

"Let's not look back or remember now, Marta!" he said. "Let's look ahead."

She nestled closer inside his arm. "Yes, Rance. Let's look ahead."

THE MAN WHO
SAW THE FUTURE

Jean de Marselait, Inquisitor Extraordinary of the King of France, raised his head from the parchments that littered the crude desk at which he sat. His glance shifted along the long stone-walled, torchlit room to the file of mail-clad soldiers who stood like steel statues by its door. A word from him and two of them sprang forward.

"You may bring in the prisoner," he said.

The two disappeared through the door, and in moments there came a clang of opening bolts and grating of heavy hinges from somewhere in the building. Then the clang of the returning soldiers, and they entered the room with another man between them whose hands were fettered.

He was a straight figure, and was dressed in drab tunic and hose. His dark hair was long and straight, and his face held a dreaming strength, altogether different from the battered visages of the soldiers or the changeless mask of the Inquisitor. The latter regarded the prisoner for a moment, and then lifted one of the parchments from before him and read from it in a smooth, clear voice.

"Henri Lothiere, apothecary's assistant of Paris," he read, "is charged in this year of our lord one thousand four hundred and forty-four with offending against God and the king by committing the crime of sorcery."

The prisoner spoke for the first time, his voice low but steady. "I am no sorcerer, sire."

Jean de Marselait read calmly on from the parchment. "It is stated by many witnesses that for long that part of Paris, called Nanley by some, has been troubled by works of the devil. Ever and anon great claps of thunder have been heard issuing from an open field there without visible cause. They were evidently caused by a sorcerer of power since even exorcists could not halt them.

"It is attested by many that the accused, Henri Lothiere, did in spite of the known diabolical nature of the thing, spend much time at the field in question. It is also attested that the said Henri

Lothiere did state that in his opinion the thunderclaps were not of diabolical origin, and that if they were studied, their cause might be discovered.

"It being suspected from this that Henri Lothiere was himself the sorcerer causing the thunderclaps, he was watched and on the third day of June was seen to go in the early morning to the unholy spot with certain instruments. There he was observed going through strange and diabolical conjurations, when there came suddenly another thunderclap and the said Henri Lothiere did vanish entirely from view in that moment. This fact is attested beyond all doubt.

"The news spreading, many hundreds watched around the field during that day. Upon that night before midnight, another thunderclap was heard and the said Henri Lothiere was seen by these hundreds to appear at the field's center as swiftly and as strangely as he had vanished. The fear-stricken hundreds around the field heard him tell them how, by diabolical power, he had gone for hundreds of years into the future, a thing surely possible only to the devil and his minions, and heard him tell other blasphemies before they seized him and brought him to the Inquisitor of the King, praying that he be burned and his work of sorcery thus halted.

"Therefore, Henri Lothiere, since you were seen to vanish and to reappear as only the servants of the evil one might do, and were heard by many to utter the blasphemies mentioned, I must adjudge you a sorcerer with the penalty of death by fire. If anything there be that you can advance in palliation of your black offense, however, you may now do so before final sentence is passed upon you."

Jean de Marselait laid down the parchment, and raised his eyes to the prisoner. The latter looked round him quickly for a moment, a half-glimpsed panic for an instant in his eyes, then seemed to steady.

"Sire, I cannot change the sentence you will pass upon me," he said quietly, "yet do I wish well to relate once, what happened to me and what I saw. Is it permitted me to tell that from first to last?"

The Inquisitor's head bent, and Henri Lothiere spoke, his voice gaining in strength and fervor as he continued.

"Sire, I, Henri Lothiere, am no sorcerer but a simple apothecary's assistant. It was always my nature, from earliest youth, to desire to delve into matters unknown to men; the secrets of the earth and sea and sky, the knowledge hidden from us. I knew well that this was wicked, that the Church teaches all we need to know and that heaven frowns when we pry into its mysteries, but so strong was my desire to know, that many times I concerned myself with matters forbidden.

"I had sought to know the nature of the lightning, and the manner of flight of the birds, and the way in which fishes are able to live beneath the waters, and the mystery of the stars. So when these thunderclaps began to be heard in the part of Paris in which I lived, I did not fear them so much as my neighbors. I was eager to learn only what was causing them, for it seemed to me that their cause might be learned.

"So I began to go to that field from which they issued, to study them. I waited in it and twice I heard the great thunderclaps myself. I thought they came from near the field's center, and I studied that place. But I could see nothing there that was causing them. I dug in the ground, I looked up for hours into the sky, but there was nothing. And still, at intervals, the thunderclaps sounded.

"I still kept going to the field, though I knew that many of my neighbors whispered that I was engaged in sorcery. Upon that morning of the third day of June, it had occurred to me to take certain instruments, such as loadstones, to the field, to see whether anything might be learned with them. I went, a few superstitious ones following me at a distance. I reached the field's center, and started the examinations I had planned. Then came suddenly another thunderclap and with it I passed from the sight of those who had followed and were watching, vanished from view.

"Sire, I cannot well describe what happened in that moment. I heard the thunderclap come as though from all the air around me, stunning my ears with its terrible burst of sound. And at the same moment that I heard it, I was buffeted as though by awful winds and seemed falling downward through terrific depths. Then through the hellish uproar, I felt myself bumping upon a hard surface, and the sounds quickly ceased from about me.

"I had involuntarily closed my eyes at the great thunderclap, but now, slowly, I opened them. I looked around me, first in stupefaction, and then in growing amazement. For I was not in that familiar field at all, sire, that I had been in a moment before. I was in a room, lying upon its floor, and it was such a room as I had never seen before.

"Its walls were smooth and white and gleaming. There were windows in the walls, and they were closed with sheets of glass so smooth and clear that one seemed looking through a clear opening rather than through glass. The floor was of stone, smooth and seamless as though carven from one great rock, yet seeming not, in some way, to be stone at all. There was a great circle of smooth metal inset in it, and it was on it that I was lying.

"All around the room were many great things the like of which I had never seen. Some seemed of black metal, seemed contrivances or machines of some sort. Black cords of wire connected them to each other and from part of them came a humming sound that did not stop. Others had glass tubes fixed on the front of them, and there were square black plates on which were many shining little handles and buttons.

"There was a sound of voices, and I turned to find that two men were bending over me. They were men like myself, yet they were at the same time like no men I had ever met! One was white-bearded and the other plump and bare of face. Neither of them wore cloak or tunic or hose. Instead they wore loose and straight-hanging garments of cloth.

"They were both greatly excited, it seemed, and were talking to each other as they bent over me. I caught a word or two of their speech in a moment, and found it was French they were talking. But it was not the French I knew, being so strange and with so many new words as to be almost a different language. I could understand the drift, though, of what they were saying.

"'We have succeeded!' the plump one was shouting excitedly. 'We've brought someone through at last!'

"'They will never believe it,' the other replied. 'They'll say it was faked.'

"'Nonsense!' cried the first. 'We can do it again, Rastin; we can show them before their own eyes!'

"They bent toward me, seeing me staring at them.

"'Where are you from?' shouted the plump-faced one. 'What time — what year — what century?'

"'He doesn't understand, Thicourt,' muttered the white-bearded one. 'What year is this now, my friend?' he asked me.

"I found voice to answer. 'Surely, sirs, whoever you be, you know that this is the year fourteen hundred and forty-four,' I said.

"That set them off again into a babble of excited talk, of which I could make out only a word here and there. They lifted me up, seeing how sick and weak I felt, and seated me in a strange, but very comfortable chair. I felt dazed. The two were still talking excitedly, but finally the white-bearded one, Rastin, turned to me. He spoke to me, very slowly, so that I understood him clearly, and he asked me my name. I told him.

"'Henri Lothiere,' he repeated. 'Well, Henri, you must try to understand. You are not now in the year 1444. You are five hundred years in the future, or what would seem to you the future. This is the year 1944.'

"'And Rastin and I have jerked you out of your own time across five solid centuries,' said the other, grinning.

"I looked from one to the other. 'Messieurs,' I pleaded, and Rastin shook his head.

"'He does not believe,' he said to the other. Then to me, 'Where were you just before you found yourself here, Henri?' he asked.

"'In a field at the outskirts of Paris,' I said.

"'Well, look from that window and see if you still believe yourself in your 15th-century Paris.'

"I went to the window. I looked out. Mother of God, what a sight before my eyes! The familiar gray little houses, the open fields behind them, the saunterers in the dirt streets — all these were gone and it was a new and terrible city that lay about me! Its broad streets were of stone and great buildings of many levels rose on either side of them. Great numbers of people, dressed like the two beside me, moved in the streets and also strange vehicles or carriages, undrawn by horse or ox, that rushed to and fro at undreamed-of speed! I staggered back to the chair.

"'You believe now, Henri?' asked the whitebeard, Rastin, kindly enough, and I nodded weakly. My brain was whirling.

"He pointed to the circle of metal on the floor and the machines around the room. 'Those are what we used to jerk you from your own time to this one,' he said.

"'But how, sirs?' I asked. 'For the love of God, how is it that you can take me from one time to another? Have ye become gods or devils?'

"'Neither the one nor the other, Henri,' he answered. 'We are simply scientists, physicists — men who want to know as much as man can know and who spend our lives in seeking knowledge.'

"I felt my confidence returning. These were men such as I had dreamed might some day be. 'But what can you do with time?' I asked. 'Is not time a thing unalterable, unchanging?'

"Both shook their heads. 'No, Henri, it is not. But lately have our men of science found that out.'

"They went on to tell me of things that I could not understand. It seemed they were telling that their men of knowledge had found time to be a mere measurement, or dimension, just as length or breadth or thickness. They mentioned names with reverence that I had never heard — Einstein and De Sitter and Lorentz. I was in a maze at their words.

"They said that just as men use force to move or rotate matter from one point along the three known measurements to another, so might matter be rotated from one point in time, the fourth measurement, to another, if the right force were used. They said that their machines produced that force and applied it to the metal circle from five hundred years before to this time of theirs.

"They had tried it many times, they said, but nothing had been on the spot at that time and they had rotated nothing but the air above it from the one time to the other, and the reverse. I told them of the thunderclaps that had been heard at the spot in the field and that had made me curious. They said that they had been caused by the changing of the air above the spot from the one time to the other in their trials. I could not understand these things.

"They said then that I had happened to be on the spot when they had again turned on their force and so had been rotated out of my own time into theirs. They said that they had always hoped to get someone living from a distant time in that way, since such a man would be a proof to all the other men of knowledge of what they had been able to do.

"I could not comprehend, and they saw and told me not to

fear. I was not fearful, but excited at the things that I saw around me. I asked of those things and Rastin and Thicourt laughed and explained some of them to me as best they could. Much they said that I did not understand but my eyes saw marvels in that room of which I had never dreamed.

"They showed me a thing like a small glass bottle with wires inside, and then told me to touch a button beneath it. I did so and the bottle shone with a brilliant light exceeding that of scores of candles. I shrank back, but they laughed, and when Rastin touched the button again, the light in the glass thing vanished. I saw that there were many of these things in the ceiling.

"They showed me also a rounded black object of metal with a wheel at the end. A belt ran around the wheel and around smaller wheels connected to many machines. They touched a lever on this object and a sound of humming came from it and the wheel turned very fast, turning all the machines with the belt. It turned faster than any man could ever have turned it, yet when they touched the lever again, its turning ceased. They said that it was the power of the lightning in the skies that they used to make the light and to turn that wheel!

"My brain reeled at the wonders that they showed. One took an instrument from the table that he held to his face, saying that he would summon the other scientists or men of knowledge to see their experiment that night. He spoke into the instrument as though to different men, and let me hear voices from it answering him! They said that the men who answered were leagues separated from him!

"I could not believe — and yet somehow I did believe! I was half-dazed with wonder and yet excited too. The white-bearded man, Rastin, saw that, and encouraged me. Then they brought a small box with an opening and placed a black disk on the box, and set it turning in some way. A woman's voice came from the opening of the box, singing. I shuddered when they told me that the woman was one who had died years before. Could the dead speak thus?

"How can I describe what I saw there? Another box or cabinet there was, with an opening also. I thought it was like that from which I had heard the dead woman singing, but they said it was different. They touched buttons on it and a voice came from it speaking in a tongue I knew not. They said that the man was speaking thousands of leagues from us, in a strange land across the uncrossed western ocean, yet he seemed speaking by my side!

"They saw how dazed I was by these things, and gave me wine. At that I took heart, for wine, at least, was as it had always been.

"'You will want to see Paris — the Paris of our time, Henri?' asked Rastin.

"'But it is different — terrible — ' I said.

"'We'll take you,' Thicourt said, 'but first your clothes —'

"He got a long light coat that they had me put on, that covered my tunic and hose, and a hat of grotesque round shape that they put on my head. They led me then out of the building and into the street.

"I gazed astoundedly along that street. It had a raised walk at either side, on which many hundreds of people moved to and fro, all dressed in as strange a fashion. Many, like Rastin and Thicourt, seemed of gentle blood, yet, in spite of this, they did not wear a sword or even a dagger. There were no knights or squires, or priests or peasants. All seemed dressed much the same.

"Small lads ran to and fro selling what seemed sheets of very thin white parchment, many times folded and covered with lettering. Rastin said that these had written in them all things that had happened through all the world, even but hours before. I said that to write even one of these sheets would take a clerk many days, but they said that the writing was done in some way very quickly by machines.

"In the broad stone street between the two raised walks were rushing back and forth the strange vehicles I had seen from the window. There was no animal pulling or pushing any one of them, yet they never halted their swift rush, and carried many people at unthinkable speed. Sometimes those who walked stepped before the rushing vehicles, and then from them came terrible warning snarls or moans that made the walkers draw back.

"One of the vehicles stood at the walk's edge before us, and we entered it and sat side by side on a soft leather seat. Thicourt sat behind a wheel on a post, with levers beside him. He touched these and a humming sound came from somewhere in the vehicle and then it too began to rush forward. Faster and faster along the street it went, yet neither of them seemed afraid.

"Many thousands of these vehicles were moving swiftly through the streets about us. We passed on, between great buildings and along wider streets, my eyes and ears numbed by what I saw about me. Then the buildings grew smaller, after we had gone for miles through them, and we were passing through the city's outskirts. I could not believe, hardly, that it was Paris in which I was.

"We came to a great flat and open field outside the city and there Thicourt stopped and we got out of the vehicle. There were big buildings at the field's end, and I saw other vehicles rolling out of them across the field, ones different from any I had yet seen, with flat winglike projections on either side. They rolled out over the field very fast and then I cried out as I saw them rising from the ground into the air. Mother of God, they were flying! The men in them were flying!

"Rastin and Thicourt took me forward to the great buildings. They spoke to men there and one brought forward one of the winged cars. Rastin told me to get in, and though I was terribly afraid, there was too terrible a fascination that drew me in. Thicourt and Rastin entered after me, and we sat in seats with the other man. He had before him levers and buttons, while at the car's front was a great thing like a double-oar or paddle. A loud roaring came and that double-blade began to whirl so swiftly that I could not see it. Then the car rolled swiftly forward, bumping on the ground, and then ceased to bump. I looked down, then shuddered. The ground was already far beneath! I too, was flying in the air!

"We swept upward at terrible speed that increased steadily. The thunder of the car was terrific, and, as the man at the levers changed their position, we curved around and over downward and upward as though birds. Rastin tried to explain to me how the car flew, but it was all too wonderful, and I could not understand. I only knew that a wild thrilling excitement held me, and that it were worth life and death to fly thus, if but for once, as I had always dreamed that men might some day do.

"Higher and higher we went. The earth lay far beneath and I saw now that Paris was indeed a mighty city, its vast mass of buildings stretching away almost to the horizons below us. A mighty city of the future that it had been given my eyes to look on!

"There were other winged cars darting to and fro in the air about us, and they said that many of these were starting or finishing journeys of hundreds of leagues in the air. Then I cried out as I saw a great shape coming nearer us in the air. It was many rods in length, tapering to a point at both ends, a vast ship sailing in the air! There were great cabins on its lower part and in them we glimpsed people gazing out, coming and going inside, dancing even! They told me that vast ships of the air like this sailed to and fro for thousands of leagues with hundreds inside them.

"The huge vessel of the air passed us and then our winged car began to descend. It circled smoothly down to the field like a swooping bird, and, when we landed there, Rastin and Thicourt led me back to the ground-vehicle. It was late afternoon by then, the sun sinking westward, and darkness had descended by the time we rolled back into the great city.

"But in that city was not darkness! Lights were everywhere in it, flashing brilliant lights that shone from its mighty buildings and that blinked and burned and ran like water in great symbols upon the buildings above the streets. Their glare was like that of day! We stopped before a great building into which Rastin and Thicourt led me.

"It was vast inside and in it were many people in rows on rows of seats. I thought it a cathedral at first but saw soon that it was not. The wall at one end of it, toward which all in it were gazing, had on it pictures of people, great in size, and those pictures were moving as though themselves alive! And they were talking one to another, too, as though with living voices! I trembled. What magic!

"With Rastin and Thicourt in seats beside me, I watched the pictures enthralled. It was like looking through a great window into strange worlds. I saw the sea, seemingly tossing and roaring there before me, and then saw on it a ship, a vast ship of size incredible, without sails or oars, holding thousands of people. I seemed on that ship as I watched, seemed moving forward with it. They told me it was sailing over the western ocean that never men had crossed. I feared!

"Then another scene, land appearing from the ship. A great

statue, upholding a torch, and we on the ship seemed passing beneath it. They said that the ship was approaching a city, the city of New York, but mists hid all before us. Then suddenly the mists before the ship cleared and there before me seemed the city.

"Mother of God, what a city! Climbing range on range of great mountain-like buildings that aspired up as though to scale heaven itself! Far beneath narrow streets pierced through them and in the picture we seemed to land from the ship, to go through those streets of the city. It was an incredible city of madness! The streets and ways were mere chasms between the sky-toppling buildings! People — people — people — millions on millions of them rushed through the endless streets. Countless ground-vehicles rushed to and fro also, and other different ones that roared above the streets and still others below them!

"Winged flying-cars and great airships were sailing to and fro over the titanic city, and in the waters around it great ships of the sea and smaller ships were coming as man never dreamed of surely, that reached out from the mighty city on all sides. And with the coming of darkness, the city blazed with living light!

"The pictures changed, showed other mighty cities, though none so terrible as that one. It showed great mechanisms that appalled me. Giant metal things that scooped in an instant from the earth as much as a man might dig in days. Vast things that poured molten metal from them like water. Others that lifted loads that hundreds of men and oxen could not have stirred.

"They showed men of knowledge like Rastin and Thicourt beside me. Some were healers, working miraculous cures in a way that I could not understand. Others were gazing through giant tubes at the stars, and the pictures showed what they saw, showed that all of the stars were great suns like our sun, and that our sun was greater than earth, that earth moved around it instead of the reverse! How could such things be, I wondered. Yet they said that it was so, that earth was round like an apple, and that with other earths like it, the planets, moved round the sun. I heard, but could scarce understand.

"At last Rastin and Thicourt led me out of that place of living pictures and to their ground-vehicle. We went again through the streets to their building, where first I had found myself. As we went I saw that none challenged my right to go, nor asked who was my lord. And Rastin said that none now had lords, but that all were lord, king and priest and noble, having no more power than any in the land. Each man was his own master! It was what I had hardly dared to hope for, in my own time, and this, I thought, was greatest of all the marvels they had shown me!

"We entered again their building but Rastin and Thicourt took me first to another room than the one in which I had found myself. They said that their men of knowledge were gathered there to hear of their feat, and to have it proved to them.

"'You would not be afraid to return to your own time, Henri?' asked Rastin, and I shook my head.

"'I want to return to it,' I told them. 'I want to tell my people there what I have seen — what the future is that they must strive for.'

"'But if they should not believe you?' Thicourt asked.

"'Still I must go — must tell them,' I said.

"Rastin grasped my hand. 'You are a man, Henri,' he said. Then, throwing aside the cloak and hat I had worn outside, they went with me down to the big white-walled room where first I had found myself.

"It was lit brightly now by many of the shining glass things on ceiling and walls, and in it were many men. They all stared strangely at me and at my clothes, and talked excitedly so fast that I could not understand. Rastin began to address them.

"He seemed explaining how he had brought me from my own time to his. He used many terms and words that I could not understand, incomprehensible references and phrases, and I could understand but little. I heard again the names of Einstein and De Sitter that I had heard before, repeated frequently by these men as they disputed with Rastin and Thicourt. They seemed disputing about me.

"One big man was saying, 'Impossible! I tell you, Rastin, you have faked this fellow!'

"Rastin smiled. 'You don't believe that Thicourt and I brought him here from his own time across five centuries?'

"A chorus of excited negatives answered him. He had me stand up and speak to them. They asked me many questions, part of which I could not understand. I told them of my life, and of the city of my own time, and of king and priest and noble, and of many simple things that they seemed quite ignorant of. Some appeared to believe me but others did not, and again their dispute broke out.

"'There is a way to settle the argument, gentlemen,' said Rastin finally.

"'How?' all cried.

"'Thicourt and I brought Henri across five centuries by rotating the time-dimensions at this spot,' he said. 'Suppose we reverse that rotation and send him back before your eyes — would that be proof?'

"They all said that it would. Rastin turned to me. 'Stand on the metal circle, Henri,' he said. I did so.

"All were watching very closely. Thicourt did something quickly with the levers and buttons of the mechanisms in the room. They began to hum, and blue light came from the glass tubes on some. All were quiet, watching me as I stood there on the circle of metal. I met Rastin's eyes and something in me made me call goodbye to him. He waved his hand and smiled. Thicourt pressed more buttons and the hum of the mechanisms grew louder. Then he reached toward another lever. All in the room were tense and I was tense.

"Then I saw Thicourt's arm move as he turned one of the many levers.

"A terrific clap of thunder seemed to break around me, and as I closed my eyes before its shock, I felt myself whirling around and falling at the same time as though into a maelstrom, just as I had done before. The awful falling sensation ceased in a moment and the sound subsided. I opened my eyes. I was on the ground at the center of the familiar field from which I had vanished hours before, upon the morning of that day. It was night now, though, for that day I had spent five hundred years in the future.

"There were many people gathered around the field, fearful, and they screamed and some fled when I appeared in the thunderclap. I went toward those who remained. My mind was full of things I had seen and I wanted to tell them of these things. I wanted to tell them how they must work ever toward that future time of wonder.

"But they did not listen. Before I had spoken minutes to them they cried out on me as a sorcerer and a blasphemer, and seized me and brought me here to the Inquisitor, to you, sire.

And to you, sire, I have told the truth in all things. I know that in doing so I have set the seal of my own fate, and that only a sorcerer would ever tell such a tale, yet despite that I am glad. Glad that I have told one at least of this time of what I saw five centuries in the future. Glad that I saw! Glad that I saw the things that someday, sometime, must come to be —"

It was a week later that they burned Henri Lothiere. Jean de Marselait, lifting his gaze from his endless parchment accusation and examens on that afternoon, looked out through the window at a thick curl of black smoke going up from the distant square.

"Strange, that one," he mused. "A sorcerer, of course, but such a one as I had never heard before. I wonder," he half-whispered, "was there any truth in that wild tale of his? The future — who can say — what men might do — ?"

There was silence in the room as he brooded for a moment, and then he shook himself as one ridding himself of absurd speculations. "But tush — enough of these crazy fancies. They will have me for a sorcerer if I yield to these wild fancies and visions *of the future.*"

And bending again with his pen to the parchment before him, he went gravely on with his work.

THE STARS, MY BROTHERS

1.

Something tiny went wrong, but no one ever knew whether it was in an electric relay or in the brain of the pilot.

The pilot was Lieutenant Charles Wandek, UNRC, home address: 1677 Anstey Avenue, Detroit. He did not survive the crash of his ferry into Wheel Five. Neither did his three passengers, a young French astrophysicist, an East Indian expert on magnetic fields, and a forty-year-old man from Philadelphia who was coming out to replace a pump technician.

Someone else who did not survive was Reed Kieran, the only man in Wheel Five itself to lose his life. Kieran, who was thirty-six years old, was an accredited scientist-employee of UNRC. Home address: 815 Elm Street, Midland Springs, Ohio.

Kieran, despite the fact that he was a confirmed bachelor, was in Wheel Five because of a woman. But the woman who had sent him there was no beautiful lost love. Her name was Gertrude Lemmiken; she was nineteen years old and overweight, with a fat, stupid face. She suffered from head-colds, and sniffed constantly in the Ohio college classroom where Kieran taught Physics Two.

One March morning, Kieran could bear it no longer. He told himself, "If she sniffs this morning, I'm through. I'll resign and join the UNRC."

Gertrude sniffed. Six months later, having finished his training for the United Nations Reconnaissance Corps, Kieran shipped out for a term of duty in UNRC Space Laboratory Number 5, known more familiarly as Wheel Five.

Wheel Five circled the Moon. There was an elaborate base on the surface of the Moon in this year 1981. There were laboratories and observatories there, too. But it had been found that the alternating fortnights of boiling heat and near-absolute-zero cold on the lunar surface could play havoc with the delicate instruments used in certain researches. Hence Wheel Five had been built and was staffed by research men who were rotated at regular eight-month intervals.

Kieran loved it, from the first. He thought that that was because of the sheer beauty of it, the gaunt, silver deaths-head of the Moon forever turning beneath, the still and solemn glory of the undimmed stars, the filamentaries stretched across the distant star-clusters like shining veils, the quietness, the peace.

But Kieran had a certain intellectual honesty, and after a while he admitted to himself that neither the beauty nor the romance of it was what made this life so attractive to him. It was the fact that he was far away from Earth. He did not even have to look at Earth, for nearly all geophysical research was taken care of by Wheels Two and Three that circled the mother planet. He was almost completely divorced from all Earth's problems and people.

Kieran liked people, but had never felt that he understood them. What seemed important to them, all the drives of ordinary day-to-day existence, had never seemed very important to him. He had felt that there must be something wrong with him, something lacking, for it seemed to him that people everywhere committed the most outlandish follies, believed in the most incredible things, were swayed by pure herd-instinct into the most harmful courses of behavior. They could not all be wrong, he thought, so he must be wrong — and it had worried him. He had taken partial refuge in pure science, but the study and then the teaching of astrophysics had not been the refuge that Wheel Five was. He would be sorry to leave the Wheel when his time was up.

And he was sorry, when the day came. The others of the staff were already out in the docking lock in the rim, waiting to greet the replacements from the ferry. Kieran, hating to leave, lagged behind. Then, realizing it would be churlish not to meet this young Frenchman who was replacing him, he hurried along the corridor in the big spoke when he saw the ferry coming in.

He was two-thirds of the way along the spoke to the rim when it happened. There was a tremendous crash that flung him violently from his feet. He felt a coldness, instant and terrible.

He was dying.

He was dead.

The ferry had been coming in on a perfectly normal approach when the tiny something went wrong, in the ship or in the judgment of the pilot. Its drive-rockets suddenly blasted on full, it heeled over sharply, it smashed through the big starboard spoke like a knife through butter.

Wheel Five staggered, rocked, and floundered. The automatic safety bulkheads had all closed, and the big spoke — Section T2 — was the only section to blow its air, and Kieran was the only man caught in it. The alarms went off, and while the wreckage of the ferry, with three dead men in it, was still drifting close by, everyone in the Wheel was in his pressure-suit and emergency measures were in full force.

Within thirty minutes it became evident that the Wheel was going to survive this accident. It was edging slowly out of orbit from the impetus of the blow, and in the present weakened state of the construction its small corrective rockets could not be used to stop the drift. But Meloni, the UNRC captain commanding, had got first reports from his damage-control teams, and it did not look too bad. He fired off peremptory demands for the repair materials he would need, and was assured by UNRC headquarters at Mexico City that the ferries would be loaded and on their way as soon as possible.

Meloni was just beginning to relax a little when a young officer brought up a minor but vexing problem. Lieutenant Vinson had headed the small party sent out to recover the bodies of the four dead men. In their pressure-suits they had been pawing through the tangled wreckage for some time, and young Vinson was tired when he made his report.

"We have all four alongside, sir. The three men in the ferry were pretty badly mangled in the crash. Kieran wasn't physically wounded, but died from space-asphyxiation."

The captain stared at him. "Alongside? Why didn't you bring them in? They'll go back in one of the ferries to Earth for burial."

"But —" Vinson started to protest.

Meloni interrupted sharply. "You need to learn a few things about morale, Lieutenant. You think it's going to do morale here any good to have four dead men floating alongside where everyone can see them? Fetch them in and store them in one of the holds."

Vinson, sweating and unhappy now, had visions of a black mark on his record, and determined to make his point.

"But about Kieran, sir — he was only frozen. Suppose there was a chance to bring him back?"

"Bring him back? What the devil are you talking about?"

Vinson said, "I read they're trying to find some way of restoring a man that gets space-frozen. Some scientists down at Delhi University. If they succeeded, and if we had Kieran still intact in space —"

"Oh, hell, that's just a scientific pipe-dream, they'll never find a way to do that," Meloni said. "It's all just theory."

"Yes, sir," said Vinson, hanging his head.

"We've got trouble enough here without you bringing up ideas like this," the captain continued angrily. "Get out of here."

Vinson was now completely crushed. "Yes, sir. I'll bring the bodies in."

He went out. Meloni stared at the door, and began to think. A commanding officer had to be careful, or he could get skinned alive. If, by some remote chance, this Delhi idea ever succeeded, he, Meloni, would be in for it for having Kieran buried. He strode to the door and flung it open, mentally cursing the young snotty who had had to bring this up.

"Vinson!" he shouted.

The lieutenant turned back, startled. "Yes, sir?"

"Hold Kieran's body outside. I'll check on this with Mexico City."

"Yes, sir."

Still angry, Meloni shot a message to Personnel at Mexico City. That done, he forgot about it. The buck had been passed, let the boys sitting on their backsides down on Earth handle it.

Colonel Hausman, second in command of Personnel Division of UNRC, was the man to whom Meloni's message went. He snorted loudly when he read it. And later, when he went in to report to Garces, the brigadier commanding the Division, he took the message with him.

"Meloni must be pretty badly rattled by the crash," he said. "Look at this."

Garces read the message, then looked up. "Anything to this? The Delhi experiments, I mean?"

Hausman had taken care to brief himself on that point and was able to answer emphatically.

"Damned little. Those chaps in Delhi have been playing around freezing insects and thawing them out, and they think the process might be developed someday to where it could revive frozen spacemen. It's an iffy idea. I'll burn Meloni's backside off for bringing it up at a time like this."

Garces, after a moment, shook his head. "No, wait. Let me think about this."

He looked speculatively out of the window for a few moments. Then he said,

"Message Meloni that this one chap's body — what's his name, Kieran? — is to be preserved in space against a chance of future revival."

Hausman nearly blotted his copybook by exclaiming, "For God's sake —" He choked that down in time and said, "But it could be centuries before a revival process is perfected, if it ever is."

Garces nodded. "I know. But you're missing a psychological point that could be valuable to UNRC. This Kieran has relatives, doesn't he?"

Hausman nodded. "A widowed mother and a sister. His father's been dead a long time. No wife or children."

Garces said, "If we tell them he's dead, frozen in space and then buried, it's all over with. Won't those people feel a lot better if we tell them that he's *apparently* dead, but might be brought back when a revival-technique is perfected in the future?"

"I suppose they'd feel better about it," Hausman conceded. "But I don't see —"

Garces shrugged. "Simple. We're only really beginning in space, you know. As we go on, UNRC is going to lose a number of men, space-struck just like Kieran. A howl will go up about our casualty lists, it always does. But if we can say that they're only frozen until such time as revival technique is achieved, everyone will feel better about it."

"I suppose public relations are important —" Hausman began to say, and Garces nodded quickly.

"They are. See that this is done, when you go up to confer with Meloni. Make sure that it gets onto the video networks, I want everyone to see it."

Later, with many cameras and millions of people watching, Kieran's body, in a pressure-suit, was ceremoniously taken to a selected position where it would orbit the Moon. All suggestions of the funerary were carefully avoided. The space-struck man — nobody at all referred to him as "dead" — would remain in this position until a revival process was perfected.

"Until forever," thought Hausman, watching sourly. "I suppose Garces is right. But they'll have a whole graveyard here, as time goes on."

As time went on, they did.

2.

In his dreams, a soft voice whispered.

He did not know what it was telling him, except that it was important. He was hardly aware of its coming, the times it came. There would be the quiet murmuring, and something in him seemed to hear and understand, and then the murmur faded away and there was nothing but the dreams again.

But were they dreams? Nothing had form or meaning. Light, darkness, sound, pain and not-pain, flowed over him. Flowed over — who? Who was he? He did not even know that. He did not care.

But he came to care, the question vaguely nagged him. He should try to remember. There was more than dreams and the whispering voice. There was — what? If he had one real thing to cling to, to put his feet on and climb back from — One thing like his name.

He had no name. He was no one. Sleep and forget it. Sleep and dream and listen —

"Kieran."

It went across his brain like a shattering bolt of lightning, that word. He did not know what the word was or what it meant but it found an echo somewhere and his brain screamed it.

"Kieran!"

Not his brain alone, his voice was gasping it, harshly and croakingly, his lungs seeming on fire as they expelled the word.

He was shaking. He had a body that could shake, that could feel pain, that was feeling pain now. He tried to move, to break the nightmare, to get back again to the vague dreams, and the soothing whisper.

He moved. His limbs thrashed leadenly, his chest heaved and panted, his eyes opened.

He lay in a narrow bunk in a very small metal room.

He looked slowly around. He did not know this place. The gleaming white metal of walls and ceiling was unfamiliar. There was a slight, persistent tingling vibration in everything that was unfamiliar, too.

He was not in Wheel Five. He had seen every cell in it and none of them were like this. Also, there lacked the persistent susurrant sound of the ventilation pumps. Where —

You're in a ship, Kieran. A starship.

Something back in his mind told him that. But of course it was ridiculous, a quirk of the imagination. There weren't any starships.

You're all right, Kieran. You're in a starship, and you're all right.

The emphatic assurance came from somewhere back in his brain and it was comforting. He didn't feel very good, he felt dopey and sore, but there was no use worrying about it when he knew for sure he was all right —

The hell he was all right! He was in someplace new, some-place strange, and he felt half sick and he was not all right at all. Instead of lying here on his back listening to comforting lies from his imagination, he should get up, find out what was going on, what had happened.

Of a sudden, memory began to clear. What *had* happened? Something, a crash, a terrible coldness —

Kieran began to shiver. He had been in Section T2, on his way to the lock, and suddenly the floor had risen under him and Wheel Five had seemed to crash into pieces around him. The cold, the pain —

You're in a starship. You're all right.

For God's sake why did his mind keep telling him things like that, things he believed? For if he did not believe them he would be in a panic, not knowing where he was, how he had come here. There was panic in his mind but there was a barrier against it, the barrier of the soothing reassurances that came from he knew not where.

He tried to sit up. It was useless, he was too weak. He lay, breathing heavily. He felt that he should be hysterical with fear but somehow he was not, that barrier in his mind prevented it.

He had decided to try shouting when a door in the side of the little room slid open and a man came in.

He came over and looked down at Kieran. He was a young man, sandy-haired, with a compact, chunky figure and a flat, hard face. His eyes were blue and intense, and they gave Kieran the feeling that this man was a wound-up spring. He looked down and said,

"How do you feel, Kieran?"

Kieran looked up at him. He asked, "Am I in a starship?"

"Yes."

"But there aren't any starships."

"There are. You're in one." The sandy-haired man added, "My name is Vaillant."

It's true, what he says, murmured the something in Kieran's mind.

"Where — how —" Kieran began.

Vaillant interrupted his stammering question. "As to where, we're quite a way from Earth, heading right now in the general direction of Altair. As to how —" He paused, looking keenly down at Kieran. "Don't you know how?"

Of course I know. I was frozen, and now I have been awakened and time has gone by —

Vaillant, looking searchingly down at his face, showed a trace of relief. "You do know, don't you? For a moment I was afraid it hadn't worked."

He sat down on the edge of the bunk.

"How long?" asked Kieran.

Vaillant answered as casually as though it was the most ordinary question in the world. "A bit over a century."

It was wonderful, thought Kieran, how he could take a statement like that without getting excited. It was almost as though he'd known it all the time.

"How —" he began, when there was an interruption.

Something buzzed thinly in the pocket of Vaillant's shirt. He took out a thin three-inch disk of metal and said sharply into it,

"Yes?"

A tiny voice squawked from the disk. It was too far from

Kieran for him to understand what it was saying but it had a note of excitement, almost of panic, in it.

Something changed, hardened, in Vaillant's flat face. He said, "I expected it. I'll be right there. You know what to do."

He did something to the disk and spoke into it again. "Paula, take over here."

He stood up. Kieran looked up at him, feeling numb and stupid. "I'd like to know some things."

"Later," said Vaillant. "We've got troubles. Stay where you are."

He went rapidly out of the room. Kieran looked after him, wondering. Troubles — troubles in a starship? And a century had passed —

He suddenly felt an emotion that shook his nerves and tightened his guts. It was beginning to hit him now. He sat up in the bunk and swung his legs out of it and tried to stand but could not, he was too weak. All he could do was to sit there, shaking.

His mind could not take it in. It seemed only minutes ago that he had been walking along the corridor in Wheel Five. It seemed that Wheel Five must exist, that the Earth, the people, the time he knew, must still be somewhere out there. This could be some kind of a joke, or some kind of psychological experiment. That was it — the space-medicine boys were always making way-out experiments to find out how men would bear up in unusual conditions, and this must be one of them —

A woman came into the room. She was a dark woman who might have been thirty years old, and who wore a white shirt and slacks. She would, he thought, have been good-looking if she had not looked so tired and so edgy.

She came over and looked down at him and said to him,

"Don't try to get up yet. You'll feel better very soon."

Her voice was a slightly husky one. It was utterly familiar to Kieran, and yet he had never seen this woman before. Then it came to him.

"You were the one who talked to me," he said, looking up at her. "In the dreams, I mean."

She nodded. "I'm Paula Ray and I'm a psychologist. You had to be psychologically prepared for your awakening."

"Prepared?"

The woman explained patiently. "Hypnopedic technique — establishing facts in the subconscious of a sleeping patient. Otherwise, it would be too terrific a shock for you when you awakened. That was proved when they first tried reviving space-struck men, forty or fifty years ago."

The comfortable conviction that this was all a fake, an experiment of some kind, began to drain out of Kieran. But if it was true —

He asked, with some difficulty, "You say that they found out how to revive space-frozen men, that long ago?"

"Yes."

"Yet it took forty or fifty years to get around to reviving me?"

The woman sighed. "You have a misconception. The process of revival was perfected that long ago. But it has been used only immediately after a wreck or disaster. Men or women in the old space-cemeteries have not been revived."

"Why not?" he asked carefully.

"Unsatisfactory results," she said. "They could not adjust psychologically to changed conditions. They usually became unbalanced. Some suicides and a number of cases of extreme schizophrenia resulted. It was decided that it was no kindness to the older space-struck cases to bring them back."

"But you brought me back?"

"Yes."

"Why?"

"There were good reasons." She was, clearly, evading that question. She went on quickly. "The psychological shock of awakening would have been devastating, if you were not prepared. So, while you were still under sedation, I used the hypnopedic method on you. Your unconscious was aware of the main facts of the situation before you awoke, and that cushioned the shock."

Kieran thought of himself, lying frozen and dead in a graveyard that was space, bodies drifting in orbit, circling slowly around each other as the years passed, in a macabre sarabande — A deep shiver shook him.

"Because all space-struck victims were in pressure-suits, dehydration was not the problem it could have been," Paula was saying. "But it's still a highly delicate process —"

He looked at her and interrupted roughly. "What reasons?"

And when she stared blankly, he added, "You said there were good reasons why you picked me for revival. What reasons?"

Her face became tight and alert. "You were the oldest victim, in point of date. That was one of the determining factors —"

"Look," said Kieran. "I'm not a child, nor yet a savage. You can drop the patronizing professional jargon and answer my question."

Her voice became hard and brittle. "You're new to this environment. You wouldn't understand if I told you."

"Try me."

"All right," she answered. "We need you, as a symbol, in a political struggle we're waging against the Sakae."

"The Sakae?"

"I told you that you couldn't understand yet," she answered impatiently, turning away. "You can't expect me to fill you in on a whole world that's new to you, in five minutes."

She started toward the door. "Oh, no," said Kieran. "You're not going yet."

He slid out of the bunk. He felt weak and shaky but resentment energized his flaccid muscles. He took a step toward her.

The lights suddenly went dim, and a bull-throated roar sounded from somewhere, an appalling sound of raw power. The slight tingling that Kieran had felt in the metal fabric around him abruptly became a vibration so deep and powerful that it dizzied him and he had to grab the stanchion of the bunk to keep from falling.

Alarm had flashed into the woman's face. Next moment, from some hidden speaker in the wall, a male voice yelled sharply,

"Overtaken — prepare for extreme evasion —"

"Get back into the bunk," she told Kieran.

"What is it?"

"It may be," she said with a certain faint viciousness, "that you're about to die a second time."

3.

The lights dimmed to semi-darkness, and the deep vibration grew worse. Kieran clutched the woman's arm.

"What's happening?"

"Damn it, let me go!" she said.

The exclamation was so wholly familiar in its human angriness that Kieran almost liked her, for the first time. But he continued to hold onto her, although he did not feel that with his present weakness he could hold her long.

"I've a right to know," he said.

"All right, perhaps you have," said Paula. "We — our group — are operating against authority. We've broken laws, in going to Earth and reviving you. And now authority is catching up to us."

"Another ship? Is there going to be a fight?"

"A fight?" She stared at him, and shock and then faint repulsion showed in her face. "But of course, you come from the old time of wars, you would think that —"

Kieran got the impression that what he had said had made her look at him with the same feelings he would have had when he looked at a decent, worthy savage who happened to be a cannibal.

"I always felt that bringing you back was a mistake," she said, with a sharpness in her voice. "Let me go."

She wrenched away from him and before he could stop her she had got to the door and slid it open. He woke up in time to lurch after her and he got his shoulder into the door-opening before she could slide it shut.

"Oh, very well, since you insist I'm not going to worry about you," she said rapidly, and turned and hurried away.

Kieran wanted to follow her but his knees were buckling under him. He hung to the side of the door-opening. He felt angry, and anger was all that kept him from falling over. He would not faint, he told himself. He was not a child, and would not be treated like one —

He got his head outside the door. There was a long and very narrow corridor out there, blank metal with a few closed doors along it. One door, away down toward the end of the corridor, was just sliding shut.

He started down the corridor, steadying himself with his hand against the smooth wall. Before he had gone more than a few steps, the anger that pushed him began to ebb away. Of a sudden, the mountainous and incredible fact of his being here, in this place, this time, this ship, came down on him like an avalanche from which the hypnopedic pre-conditioning would no longer protect him.

I am touching a starship, I am in a starship, I, Reed Kieran of Midland Springs, Ohio. I ought to be back there, teaching my classes, stopping at Hartnett's Drug Store for a soft drink on the way home, but I am here in a ship fleeing through the stars . . .

His head was spinning and he was afraid that he was going to go out again. He found himself at the door and slid it open and fell rather than walked inside. He heard a startled voice.

This was a bigger room. There was a table whose top was translucent and which showed a bewildering mass of fleeting symbols in bright light, ever changing. There was a screen on one wall of the room and that showed nothing, a blank, dark surface.

Vaillant and Paula Ray and a tall, tough-looking man of middle age were around the table and had looked up, surprised.

Vaillant's face flashed irritation. "Paula, you were supposed to keep him in his cabin!"

"I didn't think he was strong enough to follow," she said.

"I'm not," said Kieran, and pitched over.

The tall middle-aged man reached and caught him before he hit the floor, and eased him into a chair.

He heard, as though from a great distance, Vaillant's voice saying irritatedly, "Let Paula take care of him, Webber. Look at this — we're going to cross another —"

There were a few minutes then when everything was very jumbled up in Kieran's mind. The woman was talking to him. She was telling him that they had prepared him physically, as well as psychologically, for the shock of revival, and that he would be quite all right but had to take things more slowly.

He heard her voice but paid little attention. He sat in the chair and blankly watched the two men who hung over the table and its flow of brilliant symbols. Vaillant seemed to tighten up more and more as the moments passed, and there was still about him the look of a coiled spring but now the spring seemed to be wound to the breaking-point. Webber, the tall man with the tough face, watched the fleeting symbols and his face was stony.

"Here we go," he muttered, and both he and Vaillant looked up at the blank black screen on the wall.

Kieran looked too. There was nothing. Then, in an instant, the blackness vanished from the screen and it framed a vista of such cosmic, stunning splendor that Kieran could not grasp it.

Stars blazed like high fires across the screen, loops and chains and shining clots of them. This was not too different from the way they had looked from Wheel Five. But what was different was that the starry firmament was partly blotted out by vast rifted ramparts of blackness, ebon cliffs that went up to infinity. Kieran had seen astronomical photographs like this and knew what the blackness was.

Dust. A dust so fine that its percentage of particles in space would be a vacuum, on Earth. But, here where it extended over parsecs of space, it formed a barrier to light. There was a narrow rift here between the titan cliffs of darkness and he — the ship he was in — was fleeing across that rift.

The screen abruptly went black again. Kieran remained sitting and staring at it. That incredible fleeting vision had finally impressed the utter reality of all this upon his mind. They, this ship, were far from Earth — very far, in one of the dust-clouds in which they were trying to lose pursuers. This was real.

"— will have got another fix on us as we crossed, for sure," Vaillant was saying, in a bitter voice. "They'll have the net out for us — the pattern will be shaping now and we can't slip through it."

"We can't," said Webber. "The ship can't. But the flitter can, with luck."

They both looked at Kieran. "He's the important one," Webber said. "If a couple of us could get him through —"

"No," said Paula. "We couldn't. As soon as they caught the ship and found the flitter gone, they'd be after him."

"Not to Sako," said Webber. "They'd never figure that we'd take him to Sako."

"Do I have a word in this?" asked Kieran, between his teeth.

"What?" asked Vaillant.

"This. The hell with you all. I'll go no place with you or for you."

He got a savage satisfaction from saying it, he was tired of sitting there like a booby while they discussed him, but he did not get the reaction from them he had expected. The two men merely continued to look thoughtfully at him. The woman sighed,

"You see? There wasn't time enough to explain it to him. It's natural for him to react with hostility."

"Put him out, and take him along," said Webber.

"No," said Paula sharply. "If he goes out right now he's liable to stay out. I won't answer for it."

"Meanwhile," said Vaillant with an edge to his voice, "the pattern is forming up. Have you any suggestions, Paula?"

She nodded. "This."

She suddenly squeezed something under Kieran's nose, a small thing that she had produced from her pocket without his noticing it, in his angry preoccupation with the two men. He smelled a sweet, refreshing odor and he struck her arm away.

"Oh, no, you're not giving me any more dopes —" Then he stopped, for suddenly it all seemed wryly humorous to him. "A bunch of bloody incompetents," he said, and laughed. "This is the one thing I would never have dreamed — that a man could sleep, and wake up in a starship, and find the starship manned by blunderers."

"Euphoric," said Paula, to the two men.

"At that," said Webber sourly, "there may be something in what he says about us."

Vaillant turned on him and said fiercely, "If that's what you think —" Then he controlled himself and said tightly, "Quarrelling's no good. We're in a box but we can maybe still put it over if we get this man to Sako. Webber, you and Paula take him in the flitter."

Kieran rose to his feet. "Fine," he said gaily. "Let us go in the flitter, whatever that is. I am already bored with starships."

He felt good, very good. He felt a little drunk, not enough to impede his mental processes but enough to give him a fine devil-may-care indifference to what happened next. So it was only the spray Paula had given him — it still made his body feel better and removed his shock and worry and made everything seem suddenly rather amusing.

"Let us to Sako in the flitter," he said. "After all, I'm living on velvet, I might as well see the whole show. I'm sure that Sako, wherever it is, will be just as full of human folly as Earth was."

"He's euphoric," Paula said again, but her face was stricken.

"Of all the people in that space-cemetery, we had to pick one who thinks like that," said Vaillant, with a sort of restrained fury.

"You said yourself that the oldest one would be the best," said Webber. "Sako will change him."

Kieran walked down the corridor with Webber and Paula and he laughed as he walked. They had brought him back from nothingness without his consent, violating the privacy of death or near-death, and now something that he had just said had bitterly disappointed them.

"Come along," he said buoyantly to the two. "Let us not lag. Once aboard the flitter and the girl is mine."

"Oh for God's sake shut up," said Webber.

4.

It was ridiculous to be flying the stars with a bad hangover, but Kieran had one. His head ached dully, he had an unpleasant metallic taste in his mouth, and his former ebullience had given way to a dull depression. He looked sourly around.

He sat in a confined little metal coop of a cabin, hardly enough in which to stand erect. Paula Ray, in a chair a few feet away was sleeping, her head on her breast. Webber sat forward, in what appeared to be a pilot-chair with a number of crowded control banks in front of it. He was not doing anything to the controls. He looked as though he might be sleeping, too.

That was all — a tiny metal room, blank metal walls, silence. They were, presumably, flying between the stars at incredible speeds but there was nothing to show it. There were no screens such as the one he had seen in the ship, to show by artful scanning devices what vista of suns and darknesses lay outside.

"A flitter," Webber had informed him, "just doesn't have room for the complicated apparatus that such scanners require. Seeing is a luxury you dispense with in a flitter. We'll see when we get to Sako."

After a moment he had added, "If we get to Sako."

Kieran had merely laughed then, and had promptly gone to sleep. When he had awakened, it had been with the euphoria all gone and with his present hangover.

"At least," he told himself, "I can truthfully say that this one wasn't my fault. That blasted spray —"

He looked resentfully at the sleeping woman in the chair. Then he reached and roughly shook her shoulder.

She opened her eyes and looked at him, first sleepily and then with resentment.

"You had no right to wake me up," she said.

Then, before Kieran could retort, she seemed to realize the monumental irony of what she had just said, and she burst into laughter.

"I'm sorry," she said. "Go ahead and say it. I had no right to wake *you* up."

"Let's come back to that," said Kieran after a moment. "Why did you?"

Paula looked at him ruefully. "What I need now is a ten-volume history of the last century, and time enough for you to read it. But since we don't have either —" She broke off, then after a pause asked, "Your date was 1981, wasn't it? It and your name were on the tag of your pressure-suit."

"That's right."

"Well, then. Back in 1981, it was expected that men would spread out to the stars, wasn't it?"

Kieran nodded. "As soon as they had a workable high-speed drive. Several drives were being experimented with even then."

"One of them — the Flournoy principle — was finally made workable," she said. She frowned. "I'm trying to give you this briefly and I keep straying into details."

"Just tell me why you woke me up."

"I'm *trying* to tell you." She asked candidly, "Were you always so damned hateful or did the revivification process do this to you?"

Kieran grinned. "All right. Go ahead."

"Things happened pretty much as people foresaw back in 1981," she said. "The drive was perfected. The ships went out to the nearer stars. They found worlds. They established colonies from the overflowing population of Earth. They found human indigenous races on a few worlds, all of them at a rather low technical level, and they taught them.

"There was a determination from the beginning to make it one universe. No separate nationalistic groups, no chance of wars. The governing council was set up at Altair Two. Every world was represented. There are twenty-nine of them, now. It's expected to go on like that, till there are twenty-nine hundred starworlds represented there, twenty-nine thousand — any number. But —"

Kieran had been listening closely. "But what? What upset this particular utopia?"

"Sako."

"This world we're going to?"

"Yes," she said soberly. "Men found something different about this world when they reached it. It had people — human people — on it, very low in the scale of civilization."

"Well, what was the problem? Couldn't you start teaching them as you had others?"

She shook her head. "It would take a long while. But that wasn't the real problem. It was — You see, there's another race on Sako beside the human ones, and it's a fairly civilized race. The Sakae. The trouble is — the Sakae aren't human."

Kieran stared at her. "So what? If they're intelligent —"

"You talk as though it was the simplest thing in the world," she flashed.

"Isn't it? If your Sakae are intelligent and the humans of Sako aren't, then the Sakae have the rights on that world, don't they?"

She looked at him, not saying anything, and again she had that stricken look of one who has tried and failed. Then from up forward, without turning, Webber spoke.

"What do you think now of Vaillant's fine idea, Paula?"

"It can still work," she said, but there was no conviction in her voice.

"If you don't mind," said Kieran, with an edge to his voice, "I'd still like to know what this Sako business has to do with reviving me."

"The Sakae rule the humans on that world," Paula answered. "There are some of us who don't believe they should. In the Council, we're known as the Humanity Party, because we believe that humans should not be ruled by non-humans."

Again, Kieran was distracted from his immediate question — this time by the phrase "Non-human".

"These Sakae — what are they like?"

"They're not monsters, if that's what you're thinking of," Paula said. "They're bipeds — lizardoid rather than humanoid — and are a fairly intelligent and law-abiding lot."

"If they're all that, and higher in development than the humans, why shouldn't they rule their own world?" demanded Kieran.

Webber uttered a sardonic laugh. Without turning he asked, "Shall I change course and go to Altair?"

"No!" she said. Her eyes flashed at Kieran and she spoke almost breathlessly. "You're very sure about things you just heard about, aren't you? You know what's right and you know what's wrong, even though you've only been in this time, this universe, for a few hours!"

Kieran looked at her closely. He thought he was beginning to get a glimmer of the shape of things now.

"You — all you who woke me up illegally — you belong to this Humanity Party, don't you? You did it for some reason connected with that?"

"Yes," she answered defiantly. "We need a symbol in this political struggle. We thought that one of the oldtime space pioneers, one of the humans who began the conquest of the stars, would be it. We —"

Kieran interrupted. "I think I get it. It was really considerate of you. You drag a man back from what amounts to death, for a party rally. 'Oldtime space hero condemns non-humans' — it would go something like that, wouldn't it?"

"Listen —" she began.

"Listen, hell," he said. He was hot with rage, shaking with it. "I am glad to say that you could not possibly have picked a worse symbol than me. I have no more use for the idea of the innate sacred superiority of one species over another than I had for that of one kind of man over another."

Her face changed. From an angry woman, she suddenly became a professional psychologist, coolly observing reactions.

"It's not the political question you really resent," she said. "You've wakened to a strange world and you're afraid of it, in spite of all the pre-awakening preparation we gave your subconscious. You're afraid, and so you're angry."

Kieran got a grip on himself. He shrugged. "What you say

may be true. But it doesn't change the way I feel. I will not help you one damned bit."

Webber got up from his seat and came back toward them, his tall form stooping. He looked at Kieran and then at the woman.

"We have to settle this right now," he said. "We're getting near enough to Sako to go out of drive. Are we going to land or aren't we?"

"Yes," said Paula steadily. "We're landing."

Webber glanced again at Kieran's face. "But if that's the way he feels —"

"Go ahead and land," she said.

5.

It was nothing like landing in a rocket. First there was the business referred to as "going out of drive". Paula made Kieran strap in and she said, "You may find this unpleasant, but just sit tight. It doesn't last long." Kieran sat stiff and glowering, prepared for anything and determined not to show it no matter how he felt. Then Webber did something to the control board and the universe fell apart. Kieran's stomach came up and stuck in his throat. He was falling — up? Down? Sideways? He didn't know, but whichever it was not all the parts of him were falling at the same rate, or perhaps it was not all in the same direction, he didn't know that either, but it was an exceptionally hideous feeling. He opened his mouth to protest, and all of a sudden he was sitting normally in the chair in the normal cabin and screaming at the top of his lungs.

He shut up.

Paula said, "I told you it would be unpleasant."

"So you did," said Kieran. He sat, sweating. His hands and feet were cold.

Now for the first time he became aware of motion. The flitter seemed to hurtle forward at comet-like speed. Kieran knew that this was merely an ironic little joke, because now they were proceeding at something in the range of normal velocity, whereas before their speed had been quite beyond his comprehension. But he could comprehend this. He could feel it. They were going like a bat out of hell, and somewhere ahead of them was a planet, and he was closed in, blind, a mouse in a nose-cone. His insides writhed with helplessness and the imminence of a crash. He wanted very much to start screaming again, but Paula was watching him.

In a few moments that desire became academic. A whistling shriek began faintly outside the hull and built swiftly to a point where nothing could have been heard above it. Atmosphere. And somewhere under the blind wall of the flitter a rock-hard world-face reeling and rushing, leaping to meet them —

The flitter slowed. It seemed to hang motionless, quivering faintly. Then it dropped. Express elevator in the world's tallest building, top to bottom — only the elevator is a bubble and the wind is tossing it from side to side as it drops and there is no bottom.

They hung again, bounding lightly on the unseen wind.

Then down.

And hang again.

And down.

Paula said suddenly, "Webber. Webber, I think he's dying." She began to unstrap.

Kieran said faintly, "Am I turning green?"

She looked at him, frowning. "Yes."

"A simple old malady. I'm seasick. Tell Webber to quit playing humming-bird and put this thing down."

Paula made an impatient gesture and tightened her belt again.

Hang and drop. Once more, twice more. A little rocking bounce, a light thump, motion ceased. Webber turned a series of switches. Silence.

Kieran said, "Air?"

Webber opened a hatch in the side of the cabin. Light poured in. It had to be sunlight, Kieran knew, but it was a queer color, a sort of tawny orange that carried a pleasantly burning heat. He got loose with Paula helping him and tottered to the hatch. The air smelled of clean sun-warmed dust and some kind of vegetation. Kieran climbed out of the flitter, practically throwing himself out in his haste. He wanted solid ground under him, he didn't care whose or where.

And as his boots thumped onto the red-ochre sand, it occurred to him that it had been a very long time since he had had solid ground underfoot. A very long time indeed —

His insides knotted up again, and this time it was not seasickness but fear, and he was cold all through again in spite of the hot new sun.

He was afraid, not of the present, nor of the future, but of the past. He was afraid of the thing tagged Reed Kieran, the stiff blind voiceless thing wheeling its slow orbit around the Moon, companion to dead worlds and dead space, brother to the cold and the dark.

He began to tremble.

Paula shook him. She was talking but he couldn't hear her. He could only hear the rush of eternal darkness past his ears, the thin squeak of his shadow brushing across the stars. Webber's face was somewhere above him, looking angry and disgusted. He was talking to Paula, shaking his head. They were far away. Kieran was losing them, drifting away from them on the black tide. Then suddenly there was something like an explosion, a crimson flare across the black, a burst of heat against the cold. Shocked and wild, the physical part of him clawed back to reality.

Something hurt him, something threatened him. He put his hand to his cheek and it came away red.

Paula and Webber were yanking at him, trying to get him to move.

A stone whizzed past his head. It struck the side of the flitter with a sharp clack, and fell. Kieran's nervous relays finally connected. He jumped for the open hatch. Automatically he pushed Paula ahead of him, trying to shield her, and she gave him an odd startled look. Webber was already inside. More stones rattled around and one grazed Kieran's thigh. It hurt. His cheek was bleeding freely. He rolled inside the flitter and turned to look back out the hatch. He was mad.

"Who's doing it?" he demanded.

Paula pointed. At first Kieran was distracted by the strangeness of the landscape. The flitter crouched in a vastness of red-ochre sand laced with some low-growing plant that shone like metallic gold in the sunlight. The sand receded in tilted planes lifting gradually to a range of mountains on the right, and dropping gradually to infinity on the left. Directly in front of the flitter and quite literally a stone's throw away was the beginning of a thick belt of trees that grew beside a river, apparently quite a wide one though he could not see much but a tawny sparkling of water. The course of the river could be traced clear back to the mountains by the winding line of woods that followed its bed. The trees themselves were not like any Kieran had seen before. There seemed to be several varieties, all grotesque in shape and exotic in color. There were even some green ones, with long sharp leaves that looked like spearheads.

Exotic or not, they made perfectly adequate cover. Stones came whistling out of the woods, but Kieran could not see anything where Paula was pointing but an occasional shaking of foliage.

"Sakae?" he asked.

Webber snorted. "You'll know it when the Sakae find us. They don't throw stones."

"These are the humans," Paula said. There was an indulgent softness in her voice that irritated Kieran.

"I thought they were our dear little friends," he said.

"You frightened them."

"*I* frightened them?"

"They've seen the flitter before. But they're extremely alert to modes of behavior, and they knew you weren't acting right. They thought you were sick."

"So they tried to kill me. Nice fellows."

"Self-preservation," Webber said. "They can't afford the luxury of too much kindness."

"They're very kind among themselves," Paula said defensively. To Kieran she added, "I doubt if they were trying to kill you. They just wanted to drive you away."

"Oh, well," said Kieran, "in that case I wouldn't dream of disappointing them. Let's go."

Paula glared at him and turned to Webber. "Talk to them."

"I hope there's time," Webber grunted, glancing at the sky. "We're sitting ducks here. Keep your patient quiet — any more of that moaning and flopping and we're sunk."

He picked up a large plastic container and moved closer to the door.

Paula looked at Kieran's cheek. "Let me fix that."

"Don't bother," he said. At this moment he hoped the Sakae,

whoever and whatever they were, would come along and clap these two into some suitable place for the rest of their lives.

Webber began to "talk".

Kieran stared at him, fascinated. He had expected words — primitive words, perhaps resembling the click-speech of Earth's stone-age survivals, but words of some sort. Webber hooted. It was a soft reassuring sound, repeated over and over, but it was not a word. The rattle of stones diminished, then stopped. Webber continued to make his hooting call. Presently it was answered. Webber turned and nodded at Paula, smiling. He reached into the plastic container and drew forth a handful of brownish objects that smelled to Kieran like dried fruit. Webber tossed these out onto the sand. Now he made a different sound, a grunting and whuffling. There was a silence. Webber made the sound again.

On the third try the people came out of the woods.

In all there were perhaps twenty-five of them. They came slowly and furtively, moving a step or two at a time, then halting and peering, prepared to run. The able-bodied men came first, with one in the lead, a fine-looking chap in early middle age who was apparently the chief. The women, the old men, and the children followed, trickling gradually out of the shadow of the trees but remaining where they could disappear in a flash if alarmed. They were all perfectly naked, tall and slender and large-eyed, their muscles strung for speed and agility rather than massive strength. Their bodies gleamed a light bronze color in the sun, and Kieran noticed that the men were beard-less and smooth-skinned. Both men and women had long hair, ranging in color from black to tawny, and very clean and glis-tening. They were a beautiful people, as deer are a beautiful people, graceful, innocent, and wild. The men came to the dried fruits which had been scattered for them. They picked them up and sniffed them, bit them, then began to eat, re-peating the grunt-and-whuffle call. The women and children and old men decided everything was safe and joined them. Webber tossed out more fruit, and then got out himself, car-rying the plastic box.

"What does he do next?" whispered Kieran to Paula. "Scratch their ears? I used to tame squirrels this way when I was a kid."

"Shut up," she warned him. Webber beckoned and she nudged him to move out of the flitter. "Slow and careful."

Kieran slid out of the flitter. Big glistening eyes swung to watch him. The eating stopped. Some of the little ones scuttled for the trees. Kieran froze. Webber hooted and whuffled some more and the tension relaxed. Kieran approached the group with Paula. There was suddenly no truth in what he was doing. He was an actor in a bad scene, mingling with impossible characters in an improbable setting. Webber making ridiculous noises and tossing his dried fruit around like a caricature of somebody sowing, Paula with her brisk professionalism all dissolved in misty-eyed fondness, himself an alien in this time and place, and these perfectly normal-appearing people behaving like orang-utans with their fur shaved off. He started to laugh and then thought better of it. Once started, he might not be able to stop.

"Let them get used to you," said Webber softly.

Paula obviously had been here before. She had begun to make noises too, a modified hooting more like a pigeon's call. Kieran just stood still. The people moved in around them, sniffing, touching. There was no conversation, no laughing or giggling even among the little girls. A particularly beautiful young woman stood just behind the chief, watching the strangers with big yellow cat-eyes. Kieran took her to be the man's daughter. He smiled at her. She continued to stare, deadpan and blank-eyed, with no answering flicker of a smile. It was as though she had never seen one before. Kieran shivered. All this silence and unresponsiveness became eerie.

"I'm happy to tell you," he murmured to Paula, "that I don't think much of your little pets?"

She could not allow herself to be sharply angry. She only said, in a whisper, "They are not pets, they are not animals. They —"

She broke off. Something had come over the naked people. Every head had lifted, every eye had turned away from the strangers. They were listening. Even the littlest ones were still.

Kieran could not hear anything except the wind in the trees.

"What —?" he started to ask.

Webber made an imperative gesture for silence. The tableau held for a brief second longer. Then the brown-haired man who seemed to be the leader made a short harsh noise. The people turned and vanished into the trees.

"The Sakae," Webber said. "Get out of sight." He ran toward the flitter. Paula grabbed Kieran's sleeve and pushed him toward the trees.

"What's going on?" he demanded as he ran.

"Their ears are better than ours. There's a patrol ship coming, I think."

The shadows took them in, orange-and-gold-splashed shadows under strange trees. Kieran looked back. Webber had been inside the flitter. Now he tumbled out of the hatch and ran toward them. Behind him the hatch closed and the flitter stirred and then took off all by itself, humming.

"They'll follow it for a while," Webber panted. "It may give us a chance to get away." He and Paula started after the running people.

Kieran balked. "I don't know why I'm running away from anybody."

Webber pulled out a snub-nosed instrument that looked enough like a gun to be very convincing. He pointed it at Kieran's middle.

"Reason one," he said. "If the Sakae catch Paula and me here we're in very big trouble. Reason two — this is a closed area, and you're with us, so *you* will be in very big trouble." He looked coldly at Kieran. "The first reason is the one that interests me most."

Kieran shrugged. "Well, now I know." He ran.

Only then did he hear the low heavy thrumming in the sky.

6.

The sound came rumbling very swiftly toward them. It was a completely different sound from the humming of the flitter, and it seemed to Kieran to hold a note of menace. He stopped in a small clearing where he might see up through the trees. He wanted a look at this ship or flier or whatever it was that had been built and was flown by non-humans.

But Webber shoved him roughly on into a clump of squat trees that were the color of sherry wine, with flat thick leaves.

"Don't move," he said.

Paula was hugging a tree beside him. She nodded to him to do as Webber said.

"They have very powerful scanners." She pointed with her chin. "Look. They've learned."

The harsh warning barks of the men sounded faintly, then were hushed. Nothing moved, except by the natural motion of the wind. The people crouched among the trees, so still that Kieran would not have seen them if he had not known they were there.

The patrol craft roared past, cranking up speed as it went. Webber grinned. "They'll be a couple of hours at least, overhauling and examining the flitter. By that time it'll be dark, and by morning we'll be in the mountains."

The people were already moving. They headed upstream, going at a steady, shuffling trot. Three of the women, Kieran noticed, had babies in their arms. The older children ran beside their mothers. Two of the men and several of the women were white-haired. They ran also.

"Do you like to see them run?" asked Paula, with a sharp note of passion in her voice. "Does it look good to you?"

"No," said Kieran, frowning. He looked in the direction in which the sound of the patrol craft was vanishing.

"Move along," Webber said. "They'll leave us far enough behind as it is."

Kieran followed the naked people through the woods, beside the tawny river. Paula and Webber jogged beside him. The shadows were long now, reaching out across the water.

Paula kept glancing at him anxiously, as though to detect any sign of weakness on his part. "You're doing fine," she said. "You should. Your body was brought back to normal strength and tone, before you ever were awakened."

"They'll slow down when it's dark, anyway," said Webber.

The old people and the little children ran strongly.

"Is their village there?" Kieran asked, indicating the distant mountains.

"They don't live in villages," Paula said. "But the mountains are safer. More places to hide."

"You said this was a closed area. What is it, a hunting preserve?"

"The Sakae don't hunt them any more."

"But they used to?"

"Well," Webber said, "a long time ago. Not for food, the Sakae are vegetarians, but —"

"But," said Paula, "they were the dominant race, and the people were simply beasts of the field. When they competed for land and food the people were hunted down or driven out." She swung an expressive hand toward the landscape beyond the trees. "Why do you think they live in this desert, scraping a miserable existence along the watercourses? It's land the Sakae didn't want. Now, of course, they have no objection to setting it aside as a sort of game preserve. The humans are protected, the Sakae tell us. They're living their natural life in their natural environment, and when we demand that a program —"

She was out of breath and had to stop, panting. Webber finished for her.

"We want them taught, lifted out of this naked savagery. The Sakae say it's impossible."

"Is it true?" asked Kieran.

"No," said Paula fiercely. "It's a matter of pride. They want to keep their dominance, so they simply won't admit that the people are anything more than animals, and they won't give them a chance to be anything more."

There was no more talking after that, but even so the three outlanders grew more and more winded and the people gained on them. The sun went down in a blaze of blood-orange light that tinted the trees in even more impossible colors and set the river briefly on fire. Then night came, and just after the darkness shut down the patrol craft returned, beating up along the winding river bed. Kieran froze under the black trees and the hair lifted on his skin. For the first time he felt like a hunted thing. For the first time he felt a personal anger.

The patrol craft drummed away and vanished. "They won't come back until daylight," Webber said.

He handed out little flat packets of concentrated food from

his pockets. They munched as they walked. Nobody said anything. The wind, which had dropped at sundown, picked up from a different quarter and began to blow again. It got cold. After a while they caught up with the people, who had stopped to rest and eat. The babies and old people for whom Kieran had felt a worried pity were in much better shape than he. He drank from the river and then sat down. Paula and Webber sat beside him, on the ground. The wind blew hard from the desert, dry and chill. The trees thrashed overhead. Against the pale glimmer of the water Kieran could see naked bodies moving along the river's edge, wading, bending, grubbing in the mud. Apparently they found things, for he could see that they were eating. Somewhere close by other people were stripping fruit or nuts from the trees. A man picked up a stone and pounded something with a cracking noise, then dropped the stone again. They moved easily in the dark, as though they were used to it. Kieran recognized the leader's yellow-eyed daughter, her beautiful slender height outlined against the pale-gleaming water. She stood up to her ankles in the soft mud, holding something tight in her two hands, eating.

The sweat dried on Kieran. He began to shiver.

"You're sure that patrol ship won't come back?" he asked.

"Not until they can see what they're looking for."

"Then I guess it's safe." He began to scramble around, feeling for dried sticks.

"What are you doing?"

"Getting some firewood."

"No." Paula was beside him in an instant, her hand on his arm, "No, you mustn't do that."

"But Webber said —"

"It isn't the patrol ship, Kieran. It's the people. They —"

"They what?"

"I told you they were low on the social scale. This is one of the basic things they have to be taught. Right now they still regard fire as a danger, something to run from."

"I see," Kieran said, and let the kindling fall. "Very well, if I can't have a fire, I'll have you. Your body will warm me." He pulled her into his arms.

She gasped, more in astonishment, he thought, than alarm. "What are you talking about?"

"That's a line from an old movie. From a number of old movies, in fact. Not bad, eh?"

He held her tight. She was definitely female. After a moment he pushed her away.

"That was a mistake. I want to be able to go on disliking you without any qualifying considerations."

She laughed, a curiously flat little sound. "Was everybody crazy in your day?" she asked. And then, "Reed —"

It was the first time she had used his given name. "What?"

"When they threw the stones, and we got back into the flitter, you pushed me ahead of you. You were guarding me. Why?"

He stared at her, or rather at the pale blur of her standing close to him. "Well, it's always been sort of the custom for the men to — But now that I think of it, Webber didn't bother."

"No," said Paula. "Back in your day women were still taking advantage of the dual standard — demanding complete equality with men but clinging to their special status. We've got beyond that."

"Do you like it? Beyond, I mean."

"Yes," she said. "It was good of you to do that, but —"

Webber said, "They're moving again. Come on."

The people walked this time, strung out in a long line between the trees and the water, where the light was a little better and the way more open. The three outlanders tagged behind, clumsy in their boots and clothing. The long hair of the people blew in the wind and their bare feet padded softly, light and swift.

Kieran looked up at the sky. The trees obscured much of it so that all he could see was some scattered stars overhead. But he thought that somewhere a moon was rising.

He asked Paula and she said, "Wait. You'll see."

Night and the river rolled behind them. The moonlight became brighter, but it was not at all like the moonlight Kieran remembered from long ago and far away. That had had a cold tranquility to it, but this light was neither cold nor tranquil. It seemed somehow to shift color, too, which made it even less adequate for seeing than the white moonlight he was used to. Sometimes as it filtered through the trees it seemed, ice-green, and again it was reddish or amber, or blue.

They came to a place where the river made a wide bend and they cut across it, clear of the trees. Paula touched Kieran's arm and pointed. "Look."

Kieran looked, and then he stopped still. The light was not moonlight, and its source was not a moon. It was a globular cluster of stars, hung in the sky like a swarm of fiery bees, a burning and pulsing of many colors, diamond-white and gold, green and crimson, peacock blue and smoky umber. Kieran stared, and beside him Paula murmured, "I've been on a lot of planets, but none of them have anything like this."

The people moved swiftly on, paying no attention at all to the sky.

Reluctantly Kieran followed them into the obscuring woods. He kept looking at the open sky above the river, waiting for the cluster to rise high so he could see it.

It was some time after this, but before the cluster rose clear of the trees, that Kieran got the feeling that something, or someone, was following them.

7.

He had stopped to catch his breath and shake an accumulation of sand out of his boots. He was leaning against a tree with his back to the wind, which meant that he was facing their back-trail, and he thought he saw a shadow move where there was nothing to cast a shadow. He straightened up with the little trip-hammers of alarm beating all over him, but he could see nothing more. He thought he might have been mistaken. Just the same, he ran to catch up with the others.

The people were moving steadily. Kieran knew that their senses were far keener than his, and they were obviously not aware of any danger other than the basic one of the Sakae. He decided that he must have been seeing things.

But an uneasiness persisted. He dropped behind again, this time on purpose, after they had passed a clearing. He stayed hidden behind a tree-trunk and watched. The cluster-light was bright now but very confusing to the eye. He heard a rustling that he did not think was wind, and he thought that something started to cross the clearing and then stopped, as though it had caught his scent.

Then he thought that he heard rustlings at both sides of the clearing, stealthy sounds of stalking that closed in toward him. Only the wind, he told himself, but again he turned to run. This time he met Paula, coming back to look for him.

"Reed, are you all right?" she asked. He caught her arm and pulled her around and made her run. "What is it? What's the matter?"

"I don't know." He hurried with her until he could see Webber ahead, and beyond him the bare backs and blowing hair of the people. "Listen," he said, "are there any predators here?"

"Yes," Paula said, and Webber turned sharply around.

"Have you seen something?"

"I don't know. I thought I did. I'm not sure."

"Where?"

"Behind us."

Webber made the harsh barking danger call, and the people stopped. Webber stood looking back the way they had come. The women caught the children and the men fell back to where Webber stood. They looked and listened, sniffing the air. Kieran listened too, but now he did not hear any rustlings except the high thrashing of the branches. Nothing stirred visibly and the wind would carry away any warning scent.

The men turned away. The people moved on again. Webber shrugged.

"You must have been mistaken, Kieran."

"Maybe. Or maybe they just can't think beyond the elementary. If they don't smell it, it isn't there. If something is after us it's coming up-wind, the way any hunting animal works. A couple of the men ought to circle around and —"

"Come on," said Webber wearily.

They followed the people beside the river. The cluster was high now, a hive of suns reflected in the flowing water, a kaleidoscopic rippling of colors.

Now the women were carrying the smaller children. The ones too large to be carried were lagging behind a little. So were the aged. Not much, yet. Kieran, conscious that he was weaker than the weakest of these, looked ahead at the dim bulk of the mountains and thought that they ought to be able to make it. He was not at all sure that he would.

The river made another bend. The trail lay across the bend, clear of the trees. It was a wide bend, perhaps two miles across the neck. Ahead, where the trail joined the river again, there was a rocky hill. Something about the outlines of the hill seemed wrong to Kieran, but it was too far away to be sure of anything. Overhead the cluster burned gloriously. The people set out across the sand.

Webber looked back. "You see?" he said. "Nothing."

They went on. Kieran was beginning to feel very tired now, all the artificial strength that had been pumped into him before his awakening was running out. Webber and Paula walked with their heads down, striding determinedly but without joy.

"What do you think now?" she asked Kieran. "Is this any way for humans to live?"

The ragged line of women and children moved ahead of them, with the men in the lead. It was not natural, Kieran thought, for children to be able to travel so far, and then he remembered that the young of non-predacious species have to be strong and fleet at an early age.

Suddenly one of the women made a harsh, shrill cry.

Kieran looked where she was looking, off to the left, to the river and the curving line of trees. A large black shadow slipped across the sand. He looked behind him. There were other shadows, coming with long easy bounds out of the trees, fanning out in a shallow crescent. They reminded Kieran of some animal he had once seen in a zoo, a partly catlike, partly doglike beast, a cheetah he thought it had been called, only the cheetah was spotted like a leopard and these creatures were black, with stiff, upstanding ears. They bayed, and the coursing began.

"Nothing," said Kieran bitterly. "I count seven."

Webber said, "My God, I —"

The people ran. They tried to break back to the river and the trees that could be climbed to safety, but the hunters turned them. Then they fled blindly forward, toward the hill. They ran with all their strength, making no sound. Kieran and Webber ran with them, with Paula between them. Webber seemed absolutely appalled.

"Where's that gun you had?" Kieran panted.

"It's not a gun, only a short-range shocker," he said. "It wouldn't stop these things. Look at them!"

They bounded, sporting around them, howling with a sound like laughter. They were as large as leopards and their eyes glowed in the cluster-light. They seemed to be enjoying themselves, as though hunting was the most delightful game in the world. One of them ran up to within two feet of Kieran and snapped at him with its great jaws, dodging agilely when he raised his arm. They drove the people, faster and faster. At first the men had formed around the women and children. But the formation began to disintegrate as the weaker ones dropped behind, and no attempt was made to keep it. Panic was stronger than instinct now. Kieran looked ahead. "If we can make it to that hill —"

Paula screamed and he stumbled over a child, a girl about five, crawling on her hands and knees. He picked her up. She bit and thrashed and tore at him, her bare little body hard as whalebone and slippery with sweat. He could not hold onto her. She kicked herself free of his hands and rushed wildly out of reach, and one of the black hunters pounced in and bore her away, shrieking thinly like a fledgling bird in the jaws of a cat.

"Oh my God," said Paula, and covered her head with her arms, trying to shut out sight and sound. He caught her and said harshly, "Don't faint, because I can't carry you." The child's mother, whichever of the women it might have been, did not look back.

An old woman who strayed aside was pulled down and dragged off, and then one of the white-haired men. The hill was closer. Kieran saw now what was wrong with it. Part of it was a building. He was too tired and too sick to be interested, except as it offered a refuge. He spoke to Webber, with great difficulty because he was winded. And then he realized that Webber had stumbled and fallen. Webber started to get up, but the hunters were on him. He was on his hands and knees facing them, screaming at them to get away from him. He had, obviously, had little or no experience with raw violence. Kieran ran back to him, with Paula close behind.

"Use your gun!" he yelled. He was afraid of the black hunters, but he was full of rage and the rage outweighed the fear. He yelled at them, cursing them. He hurled sand into their eyes, and one that was creeping up on Webber from the side he kicked. The creature drew off a little, not frightened but surprised. They were not used to this sort of thing from humans. "Your gun!" Kieran roared again, and Webber pulled the snub-nosed thing out of his pocket. He stood up and said unsteadily, "I told you, it's not a gun. It won't kill anything. I don't think — "

"Use it," said Kieran. "And get moving again. Slowly."

They started to move, and then across the sky a great iron voice spoke like thunder. "Lie down," it said, "please. Lie down flat."

Kieran turned his head, startled. From the direction of the building on the hill a vehicle was speeding toward them.

"The Sakae," said Webber with what was almost a sob of relief. "Lie down."

As he did so, Kieran saw a pale flash shoot out from the vehicle and knock over a hunter still hanging on the flanks of the fleeing people. He hugged the sand. Something went whining and whistling over him, there was a thunk and a screech. It was repeated, and then the iron voice spoke again.

"You may get up now. Please remain where you are." The vehicle was much closer. They were bathed in sudden light. The voice said, "Mr. Webber, you are holding a weapon. Please drop it."

"It's only a little shocker," Webber said, plaintively. He dropped it.

The vehicle had wide tracks that threw up clouds of sand. It came clanking to a halt. Kieran, shading his eyes, thought he distinguished two creatures inside, a driver and a passenger.

The passenger emerged, climbing with some difficulty over the steep step of the track, his tail rattling down behind him like a length of thick cable. Once on the ground he became quite agile, moving with a sort of oddly graceful prance on his powerful legs. He approached, his attention centered on Kieran. But he observed the amenities, placing one delicate hand on his breast and making a slight bow.

"Doctor Ray." His muzzle, shaped something like a duck's bill, nevertheless formed Paula's name tolerably well. "And you, I think, are Mr. Kieran."

Kieran said, "Yes." The star-cluster blazed overhead. The dead beasts lay behind him, the people with their flying hair had run on beyond his sight. He had been dead for a hundred years and now he was alive again. Now he was standing on alien soil, facing an alien form of life, communicating with it, and he was so dog-tired and every sensory nerve was so thoroughly flayed that he had nothing left to react with. He simply looked at the Saka as he might have looked at a fence-post, and said, "Yes."

The Saka made his formal little bow again. "I am Bregg." He shook his head. "I'm glad I was able to reach you in time. You people don't seem to have any notion of the amount of trouble you make for us —"

Paula, who had not spoken since the child was carried off, suddenly screamed at Bregg, "Murderer!"

She sprang at him, striking him in blind hysteria.

8.

Bregg sighed. He caught Paula in those fine small hands that seemed to have amazing strength and held her, at arm's length. "Doctor Ray," he said. He shook her. "Doctor Ray." She stopped screaming. "I don't wish to administer a sedative because then you will say that I drugged you. But I will if I must."

Kieran said, "I'll keep her quiet."

He took her from Bregg. She collapsed against him and began to cry. "Murderers," she whispered. "That little girl, those old people —"

Webber said, "You could exterminate those beasts. You don't have to let them hunt the people like that. It's — it's —"

"Unhuman is the word you want," said Bregg. His voice was exceedingly weary. "Please get into the car."

They climbed in. The car churned around and sped back toward the building. Paula shivered, and Kieran held her in his arms. Webber said after a moment or two, "How did you happen to be here, Bregg?"

"When we caught the flitter and found it empty, it was obvious that you were with the people, and it became imperative to find you before you came to harm. I remembered that the trail ran close by this old outpost building, so I had the patrol ship drop us here with an emergency vehicle."

Kieran said, "You knew the people were coming this way?"

"Of course." Bregg sounded surprised. "They migrate every year at the beginning of the dry season. How do you suppose Webber found them so easily?"

Kieran looked at Webber. He asked, "Then they weren't running from the Sakae?"

"Of course they were," Paula said. "You saw them yourself, cowering under the trees when the ship went over."

"The patrol ships frighten them," Bregg said. "Sometimes to the point of stampeding them, which is why we use them only in emergencies. The people do not connect the ships with us."

"That," said Paula flatly, "is a lie."

Bregg sighed. "Enthusiasts always believe what they want to believe. Come and see for yourself."

She straightened up. "What have you done to them?"

"We've caught them in a trap," said Bregg, "and we are presently going to stick needles into them — a procedure necessitated by your presence, Doctor Ray. They're highly susceptible to imported viruses, as you should remember — one of your little parties of do-gooders succeeded in wiping out a whole band of them not too many years ago. So — inoculations and quarantine."

Lights had blazed up in the area near the building. The car sped toward them.

Kieran said slowly, "Why don't you just exterminate the hunters and have done with them?"

"In your day, Mr. Kieran — yes, I've heard all about you — in your day, did you on Earth exterminate the predators so that their natural prey might live more happily?"

Bregg's long muzzle and sloping skull were profiled against the lights.

"No," said Kieran, "we didn't. But in that case, they were all animals."

"Exactly," said Bregg. "No, wait, Doctor Ray. Spare me the lecture. I can give you a much better reason than that, one even you can't quarrel with. It's a matter of ecology. The number of humans destroyed by these predators annually is negligible but they do themselves destroy an enormous number of small creatures with which the humans compete for their food. If we exterminated the hunters the small animals would multiply so rapidly that the humans would starve to death."

The car stopped beside the hill, at the edge of the lighted area. A sort of makeshift corral of wire fencing had been set up, with wide wings to funnel the people into the enclosure, where a gate was shut on them. Two Sakae were mounting guard as the party from the car approached the corral. Inside the fence Kieran could see the people, flopped around in positions of exhaustion. They did not seem to be afraid now. A few of them were drinking from a supply of water provided for them. There was food scattered for them on the ground.

Bregg said something in his own language to one of the guards, who looked surprised and questioned him, then departed, springing strongly on his powerful legs. "Wait," said Bregg.

They waited, and in a moment or two the guard came back leading one of the black hunting beasts on a chain. It was a female, somewhat smaller than the ones Kieran had fought with, and having a slash of white on the throat and chest. She howled and sprang up on Bregg, butting her great head into his shoulder, wriggling with delight. He petted her, talking to her, and she laughed doglike and licked his cheek.

"They domesticate well," he said. "We've had a tame breed for centuries."

He moved a little closer to the corral, holding tight to the animal's chain. Suddenly she became aware of the people. Instantly the good-natured pet turned into a snarling fury. She reared on her hind legs and screamed, and inside the corral the people roused up. They were not frightened now. They spat and chattered, clawing up sand and pebbles and bits of food to throw through the fence. Bregg handed the chain to the guard, who hauled the animal away by main force.

Paula said coldly, "If your point was that the people are not kind to animals, my answer is that you can hardly blame them."

"A year ago," Bregg said, "some of the people got hold of her two young ones. They were torn to pieces before they could be saved, and she saw it. I can't blame her, either."

He went on to the gate and opened it and went inside. The people drew back from him. They spat at him, too, and pelted him with food and pebbles. He spoke to them, sternly, in the tone of one speaking to unruly dogs, and he spoke words, in his own tongue. The people began to shuffle about uneasily. They stopped throwing things. He stood waiting.

The yellow-eyed girl came sidling forward and rubbed herself against his thigh, head, shoulder and flank. He reached down and stroked her, and she whimpered with pleasure and arched her back.

"Oh, for God's sake," said Kieran, "let's get out of here."

Later, they sat wearily on fallen blocks of cement inside a dusty, shadowy room of the old building. Only a hand-lamp dispelled the gloom, and the wind whispered coldly, and Bregg walked to and fro in his curious prance as he talked.

"It will be a little while before the necessary medical team can be picked up and brought here," he said. "We shall have to wait."

"And then?" asked Kieran.

"First to —" Bregg used a word that undoubtedly named a city of the Sakae but that meant nothing to Kieran, " — and then to Altair Two. This, of course, is a council matter."

He stopped and looked with bright, shrewd eyes at Kieran. "You are quite the sensation already, Mr. Kieran. The whole community of starworlds is already aware of the illegal resuscitation of one of the pioneer spacemen, and of course there is great interest." He paused. "You, yourself, have done nothing unlawful. You cannot very well be sent back to sleep, and undoubtedly the council will want to hear you. I am curious as to what you will say."

"About Sako?" said Kieran. "About — them?" He made a gesture toward a window through which the wind brought the sound of stirring, of the gruntings and whufflings of the corralled people.

"Yes. About them."

"I'll tell you how I feel," Kieran said flatly. He saw Paula and Webber lean forward in the shadows. "I'm a human man. The people out there may be savage, low as the beasts, good for nothing the way they are — but they're human. You Sakae may be intelligent, civilized, reasonable, but you're not human. When I see you ordering them around like beasts, I want to kill you. That's how I feel."

Bregg did not change his bearing, but he made a small sound that was almost a sigh.

"Yes," he said. "I feared it would be so. A man of your times — a man from a world where humans were all-dominant — would feel that way." He turned and looked at Paula and Webber. "It appears that your scheme, to this extent, was successful."

"No, I wouldn't say that," said Kieran.

Paula stood up. "But you just told us how you feel —"

"And it's the truth," said Kieran. "But there's something else." He looked thoughtfully at her. "It was a good idea. It was bound to work — a man of my time was bound to feel just this way you wanted him to feel, and would go away from here crying your party slogans and believing them. But you overlooked something —"

He paused, looking out the window into the sky, at the faint vari-colored radiance of the cluster.

"You overlooked the fact that when you awoke me, I would no longer be a man of my own time — or of any time. I was in darkness for a hundred years — with the stars my brothers, and no man touching me. Maybe that chills a man's feelings, maybe something deep in his mind lives and has time to think. I've told you how I feel, yes. But I haven't told you what I think —"

He stopped again, then said, "The people out there in the corral have my form, and my instinctive loyalty is to them. But instinct isn't enough. It would have kept us in the mud of Earth forever, if it could. Reason took us out to the wider universe. Instinct tells me that those out there are my people. Reason tells me that you —" he looked at Bregg, "— who are abhorrent to me, who would make my skin creep if I touched you, you who go by reason — that you are my real people. Instinct made a hell of Earth for millennia — I say we ought to leave it behind us there in the mud and not let it make a hell of the stars. For you'll run into this same problem over and over again as you go out into the wider universe, and the old parochial human loyalties must be altered, to solve it."

He looked at Paula and said, "I'm sorry, but if anyone asks me, that is what I'll say."

"I'm sorry, too," she said, rage and dejection ringing in her voice. "Sorry we woke you. I hope I never see you again."

Kieran shrugged. "After all, you did wake me. You're responsible for me. Here I am, facing a whole new universe, and I'll need you." He went over and patted her shoulder.

"Damn you," she said. But she did not move away from him.

FLIP THIS BOOK OVER FOR A SECOND GREAT READ!

www.ingramcontent.com/pod-product-compliance
Lightning Source LLC
Chambersburg PA
CBHW050749250626
47155CB00005B/1987

THE
COPPER-CLAD
WORLD

THE
COPPER-CLAD
WORLD

HARL VINCENT

WILDSIDE PRESS

THE COPPER-CLAD WORLD

"The Copper-Clad World" was originally published in the September, 1931 issue of *Astounding Stories* magazine.

This edition published in 2009 by Wildside Press, LLC.
www.wildsidepress.com

I

Into the Unknown

Adrift in space! Blaine Carson worked frantically at the controls, his jaw set in grim lines and his eyes narrowed to anxious slits as he peered into the diamond-studded ebon of the heavens. A million miles astern he knew the red disk of the planet Mars was receding rapidly into the blackness. And the RX8 was streaking into the outer void at a terrific pace — out of control.

Something had warned him when they left Earth; the Martian cargo of k-metal was of enormous value and a direct invitation to piracy. Of course there was the attempt at secrecy and the shippers had sent along those guards. His engineer, Tom Farley, was thoroughly reliable, too. But this failure of the control rocket-tubes, missing their destination as a result — there was something queer about it.

"Tommy," he called into the mike. "Find anything yet?"

"We-e-ll, something," the audio-phone drawled after a moment. "I'm coming up."

"What is it, Tom?" he asked when the engineer's round face appeared at the head of the engine room companionway.

Farley dropped his voice and his customary smile was gone. "I found the stern rocket-tube ignition jammed so it's firing continuously," he said; "and the others are all dead: won't fire at all. That's why she doesn't swing to the controls?"

"Can't you fix it? Lord, man, we're headed out into the belt of planetoids. We'll be wrecked."

"Nothing I can do, Blaine, without shutting down the atomic engines. Then we'd freeze to death and run out of oxygen. These ships ought to have a spare engine just to take care of the heating and air conditioning. I always said so."

"What happened to the ignition system?"

Tom Farley looked over his shoulder apprehensively. "Dirty work, Blaine," he whispered. "I'm sure of it. Tool marks on the breech of the stern tube. And there's one of those guards I don't like the looks of."

"Nonsense. The k-metal people know their men; they picked these three especially for the job."

"Who else could do it? There's only the five of us on board."

There might be something in what Tommy said, at that. A thing like this couldn't just happen by itself. And, come to think of it, one of those guards was a queer looking bird: dwarfed and hunch-backed, sort of, and with long dangling arms. It would be better to investigate.

"Get 'em up here, Tommy," Blaine said.

****

The RX8 drove on and on through the uncharted wastes outside the orbit of Mars. None of the space ships of the inner planets ever ventured out this far, and Blaine knew there was grave danger of colliding with some of the small bodies with which the zone was infested. If one of those guards was the traitor he was risking his own neck as well as theirs.

Two of them entered the control room with Tom Farley, big, husky fellows of stolid countenance and armed with regulation flame-ray pistols and gas grenades.

"Where's the other, the dwarf?" Blaine asked, his suspicions mounting immediately.

"In his bunk," Tom replied with a meaning look. "He said he'd be up in a few minutes."

The pilot-commander addressed the guards. "Fellows," he said, "I suppose you know we're in a serious fix. The ship is out of control and we've missed Mars, where your metal was to be delivered. We're speeding out into the unknown, out past the limits of space-travel toward the orbits of Jupiter, Saturn, Uranus — God knows where. And my engineer thinks that one of your number has tampered with the machinery. Know any-thing about it?" Blaine eyed them keenly.

One of the guards, Mahoney, flushed hotly. "No, sir," he snapped. "At least Kelly and meself had nothin' to do with it. But we've been suspicionin' that little Antazzo ever since we came out. It's a peculiar way he has about him, the divil."

"You think he — "

An incisive voice from the doorway way interrupted, "Never mind what he thinks, Carson. I'll do the thinking from now on."

At one man they turned to face the speaker. It was the guard, Antazzo, and he was clothed from neck to ankles in a garment of bright metallic stuff that shimmered with shifting colors like those of a soap bubble. A mask of similar stuff covered his face,

and in each hand there was a weapon resembling a ray pistol but of strangely unfamiliar design.

Mahoney shot from the hip and his stabbing ray splashed full on the hunchback's chest — but harmlessly. That lustrous garment was an insulating armor; the traitorous guard should have been shriveled to a cinder at the contact. Antazzo laughed evilly as his own weapons loosed strange and terrible energies.

Tom Farley ducked, and Blaine watched in horrified amazement as the crackling streamers of blue radiance from the dwarf's pistols found their marks. Mahoney and Kelly, standing there, bathed for a brief instant in horrid blue fire: tottering, swaying, their mouths opened wide in a last agonized effort, to cry out. Tiny pinpoints of brilliant pyrotechnics flashing and exploding within the columns of blue fire. Then, nothing! Where the two husky guards had stood there was utter emptiness; not even a shred of clothing remained. The air in the control room became heavy and acrid.

"Antazzo!" White-faced and shaking, Blaine cried out in futile protest, "My God, man, what have you done? What does this mean?"

And then, in a blaze of rage, he was on his feet. Murder was in his heart as he set himself for a crashing charge that would sweep the beast from his feet. His own flame-pistol was missing; it was a case of killing this monster with his bare hands. Tom was circling, over there, cursing horribly. One of them would get him. Strangely, Antazzo had lowered the muzzles of his pistols.

A terrific punch, started from the floor, never reached its mark. Blaine saw a tiny puff of pinkish vapor that spurted from the bosom of that metallic garment. He was coughing and gasping; helpless. Muscles refused to do his bidding. With a moan he dropped into the pilot's seat, knowing that Antazzo's will compelled him. That gas had hypnotic powers. Mechanically, his fingers strayed to the controls.

And Tom — good old Tommy — he was under the influence of the stuff too, creeping there on hands and knees toward the engine room companionway.

Antazzo was talking. "We come now to the matter of instructions," he said. "You, Farley, will assist me in restoring the ignition system to normal. You, Carson, will keep to the controls and will lay a course to Jupiter as soon as the control rocket-

tubes will respond. Understand?"

Tom growled reluctant assent from where he was crawling.

Strange, this hypnotic gas! Blaine's mind functioned clearly enough, yet he was utterly at the mercy of this madman's will — a robot of flesh and blood. "Jupiter!" he exclaimed. "Why man, it's nearly a half billion miles from the sun. Not habitable, either."

Antazzo had removed his mask and now smiled a superior smile. "We'll reach it," he said: "the RX8 is very fast. And it's not the planet itself we're bound for, but its second satellite. Io, your astronomers call this body, and it's a world sadly in need of this marvelous k-metal."

"But — but — "

"Enough!" The hunchback snarled his rebuke in Blaine's face and turned to Tom. "Come, Farley," he said, as if talking to a child, "we must get to work."

****

In a daze of conflicting emotions, Blaine turned to gaze through the forward port when the two had left the control room. The RX8 was accelerating rapidly under the steady discharge of gases from the stern rocket-tube and had already reached the speed of one thousand miles a second. If one of those tiny asteroids, even one no larger than a marble, should meet up with them it would crash through the hull plates as if they were paper. His heart went cold at the thought.

Oddly enough, he found himself *wanting* to make this trip with the demoniac Antazzo. It was the effects of the pink gas. Even with the misshapen guard down there in the engine room the power of his will was effective. The devil must be an Ionian, he thought. But how in the name of the sky-lane imps had he reached Earth? How had he wormed his way into the confidence of the k-metal people? He must have been there several years, working to this very end.

There was a tinkling crash on the starboard side amidships; a screaming swish as something slithered along the side and caromed off into the void. One of those little planetoids. Probably no bigger than a pea, and luckily they had struck it glancingly. He wiped the sudden perspiration from his forehead.

Pressure on the directive rocket controls brought no response. Would they never finish with that ignition system?

A gleaming light-fleck segregated itself from the mass of stars ahead. At first he thought he imagined it, but a second examination, this time through the telescope, convinced him it was growing larger. Drawing nearer, it was, and resolving itself into a well defined orb that was directly in their path. Fifteen hundred miles a second, the indicator read now! They'd never know what happened when they struck.

"Tommy!" he bellowed into the mike. "Are you fellows ever going to finish down there?"

There was no reply for a moment, and the blue-white globe drove madly toward them. He consulted the chart. Pallas — an asteroid some three hundred miles in diameter. Not very big as celestial bodies go, but big enough!

"Just one minute now." It was Tommy's voice coming drearily, unnaturally through the audiophone. A minute! Ninety thousand miles! It seemed the asteroid was that close already.

Antazzo was in the control room then, and the effect of his mental dominance became more pronounced. Suddenly the dwarf let out a shriek of terror when he looked through the port and saw the brilliant body that now loomed so close. Blaine experienced a savage joy in the knowledge that the hunchback was mortally afraid.

"Latza! Latza!" In his fear Antazzo lapsed into his own tongue. Then, remembering, he shouted, "We're ready, Carson. Swing wide!"

The directive rockets answered to their controls now. Quick pressure on this, a swift pull on that, swinging the energy value to maximum, brought results. The little vessel groaned and shivered under the strain as a full blast from the forward tubes retarded them. Her hull plates twisted and screeched as the steering tubes belched full energy in swinging them from their course. They were thrown forward violently, though the deceleration compensators were working to the utmost.

Pallas swung around in their field of vision, and there was a fleeting glimpse of sun-lit spires of mountains, shadowed valleys, and mysterious crevasses from which clouds of steam and yellow vapor curled. Still it seemed they must crash against one of those slender pinnacles. Nearer it came like a flash; a dizzying blur, now, that drove directly in their straining faces.

And then, abruptly, it was gone. Already thousands of miles

astern, the danger was past. Miraculously, they had escaped.

Antazzo laughed; a hollow mirthless cackle. His fingers shook crazily when he untwisted them from their grip on the port rail.

"Good work, my friend. Very good, indeed," he jabbered, his chin quivering in nervous reaction. "And now we carry on — on to Io."

Blaine Carson, almost wishing they had collided with the spire, set himself grimly to the task. He was powerless to refuse.

II

The Second Satellite

When, eventually, they swung into the orbit of Jupiter and headed in toward the enormous red-belted body, the two Earth men were heartily disgusted with the voyage and with themselves. Repeated doses of the pink gas — the ignominy of their utter subservience to the will of Antazzo — had worn them down no less than had the hard work and loss of sleep. Both were in vile humor. They endured the triumphant chatter of their captor in bitter silence.

"Over there, my friends," he said, pointing; "see? It is our destination. The golden crescent, Io, is something over a quarter million of your miles from the mother planet. See it? It is home, my friends; home to me and for yourselves in the future — if the Zara spares your lives. Lay your course to the body, Carson."

Blaine growled as he sighted through the telescope. Yet, in spite of his fury, he could not overcome the feeling of excitement that came to him when the powerful glass brought the satellite near. This body was like nothing else in the heavens. Antazzo had called it the golden crescent. Rather, it was of gleaming coppery hue, and now, as they swung around, it was fully illuminated — a brilliant sphere of unbroken contour. Smoothly globular, there was not one projection or indentation to indicate the existence of land or sea, mountain or valley, on its surface. It was like a ball of solid copper, scintillant there in the weak sunlight and the reflected light from its great mother planet.

Antazzo laughed over his absorption. "Looks peculiar to you, does it not?" he asked; "rather different from any of the bodies you have visited, you are thinking."

Blaine grunted wordless assent. The globe that was Io rushed in to meet them, growing ever larger in the field of the telescope. Now it appeared that there were tiny seams in the smooth surface, a regular criss-cross pattern of fine lines that looked like — Lord, yes, that was it! The body was constructed from an infinite number of copper plates, riveted or brazed together to form a perfect sphere.

"Why, the thing's made of copper!" Blaine gasped. "Copper

plates. It's a man-made world; artificial. But where are the inhabitants?"

Antazzo laughed uproariously. "Not man-made, my friend," he corrected, "but preserved by man for his own salvation. A dying world, it was, and the cleverest scientists in the universe saved it and themselves from certain death. What you see is merely a shell of copper, the covering they constructed to retain an atmosphere and make continuation of life possible — inside."

"Your people live *inside* that shell?" Blaine was incredulous.

"What else? We must have air to breathe and warmth for our bodies. How else could we have retained it?"

It was staggering, this revelation. The young pilot could not conceive of a completely enclosed world with inhabitants forever shut off from the light of the sun by day and from the beauties of the heavens by night. Yet here it was, drawing ever nearer, a colossal monument to the ingenuity and handiwork of a highly intelligent civilization who had labored probably for centuries to preserve their kind. A titanic task! Who could imagine a sphere of metal more than twenty-four hundred miles in diameter enclosing a world and its peoples? A copper-clad world!

They were coming in close now, and the gravitational pull of the body made itself felt. Blaine was busy with the controls, sending tremendous blasts from the forward rocket-tubes to retard their speed for a safe landing. The incredibly smooth copper surface was just beneath them, stretching miles away to the horizon in all directions.

The inductor compass was functioning. Evidently Io possessed as strong a magnetic field as did the inner planets. Antazzo now consulted a chart which he drew from his pocket, and examined minutely the surface over which they were speeding. Here and there curious designs were etched on the copper plates, and it was from these he determined their course. Obviously there was an entrance to this sealed-in world.

****

When they had proceeded some two thousand miles in a northeasterly direction Antazzo gave the order to reduce speed. Off at the horizon there appeared a bulge in the copper surface, a round protuberance that resolved itself into a great dome-shaped structure as they drew nearer. A full two hundred feet it reared itself into the heavens, and Blaine saw a number of large

circular hatches in its side that evidently covered air-locked entrances.

"You will land close by the dome, Carson," Antazzo barked, "and both of you will get into your moon-suits."

At his tone Blaine saw red. He realized on the instant that the effect of the pink gas had worn off and that he was his own master once more. All the pent-up emotions of the past few days were unleashed. If only he could get in one good punch. They might get away yet. There was plenty of k-metal to replenish the fuel supply. He whirled suddenly, muscles tensed. He faced the grinning hunchback — and was greeted by a breathtaking spurt of the pink gas. This time it was not merely a subjecting of his own will to that of the master but a complete hypnotism, a somnambulistic state. As in a dream he turned to the controls.

Now it came to him that the dwarf no longer spoke. He worked his will entirely without words; his evil mind possessed fully the mind of his victim. For Blaine Carson there was no further independent thinking. He was an automaton, a sleep-walker.

Like a detached and more or less disinterested observer, he saw that he had landed the ship. Then he noticed three dwarfs in bulky, helmeted moon-suits, shuffling clumsily across the copper plates. Hazily he knew he was with the others in an air-lock; the hiss and the throbbing of pumps told him that. Under the great dome there was the latticework of a huge reflecting telescope; strange pigmy figures scuttled here and there, working at curious machines. There was the constant purr of many motors, the gentle pulsation of floor-plates beneath his feet.

With the moon-suit removed, he realized the atmosphere was fetid and stifling. A great pressure bore on his lungs, making breathing labored and difficult. And then they were in a lift that dropped into the depths of its shaft with dizzying speed. Antazzo's grin; Tom's eyes, dull and lifeless, floating there in the haze before his own — it was all a nightmare from which he must soon awaken.

There followed a period of complete unconsciousness of movement and of his surroundings. Light — light everywhere; a blue-white radiance that beat upon his unseeing eyes with unrelenting ferocity. Stabbing pains bored into his very brain, pains

that carried with them an unspoken and unintelligible command. Why couldn't they let him alone; leave him to die in peace? He knew he was on his feet, swaying. There were voices, strident and guttural, and then by some magic the veil was lifted. His brain cleared and he saw that he stood before a dais where a much bejeweled and resplendently clad woman sat curled in the luxurious cushions of a golden seat. Chalk-white was her face and her lips crimson; amazing eyes, cat's eyes, pupils red-flecked and glittering, stared out at him.

"The Zara," Antazzo whispered. "You will make obeisance."

Mechanically, Blaine dropped to his knees and touched his forehead to the floor. Tom Farley, over there, was doing the same, but Antazzo stood erect with arms crossed over his chest and head thrown back. The eyes of the Zara swept him contemptuously from head to foot. All was not well between them.

Blaine arose from his humiliating position at a sharp command from the hunchback. Tommy did likewise and the two exchanged sheepish looks. The effects of the pink gas were wearing off once more. They were in a large hall, obviously the throne room of a palace. Men-at-arms lined the walls on either side of the dais, and these were straight limbed giants with green-bronze skin and regular features — not at all like the deformed Ionian who had captured them and stolen the RX8.

The Zara talked rapidly in throaty gutturals, her fierce gaze directed at Antazzo and her brows drawn together in a scowl that could have but one meaning. She was displeased with the hunchback, displeased and furiously angry. What was it all about? Hadn't he brought home the bacon — the k-metal they were after? Blaine was nonplused.

Then Antazzo replied to the woman who was obviously his queen. His voice rose in shrill disagreement and his scowl was as fierce as the Zara's. Threatening her, he was, the nervy devil. He clenched his fists and raised his arms in an angry gesture, pacing the floor in his fury and thrusting out a pugnacious chin while he raved. This Zara woman rose higher in her cushions, and the look that flashed from those terrible eyes would have warned a less excited human, however justifiable his anger might be. But Antazzo was in too deep to draw back, that was plain to be seen. Blaine held his breath in anticipation of an explosion.

It came then, that explosion, and in a way entirely unex-

pected and horrible to behold. The tiger woman uttered one fierce sibilant like the hiss of a serpent, a terrifying sound that silenced the hunchback and brought him stiffly to attention, mouth open and eyes bulging with horror. One of those unbelievably white arms stretched forth, threateningly tense, and a jeweled finger leveled itself at the rash Ionian. From it there flashed an intangible something that leaped to bridge the distance with the speed of light, something that screeched as it flew and crashed like breaking glass when it struck Antazzo's horrified face. In an instant he was on the floor, screaming and writhing in mortal agony.

The Zara watched with compressed lips and livid features as a host of black disk-like things covered the squirming body, spinning madly as if driven by atomic energy and emitting a myriad high-pitched tones like the angry buzzing of a swarm of bees. Antazzo's body shriveled as the things hummed on in their devilish work. Soon there was but a tiny heap of clothing with the angry black disks whirling and singing their song of hate. And then, in a puff of thick yellow vapor they were gone, their gruesome work completed. The odor of putrefaction lay heavy on the air.

Blaine shuddered and a fit of nausea twisted his vitals. It served the devil right, of course, but it was a horrible way to go. These damned Ionians, even to their queen, were bloodthirsty creatures. And what devilish ingenuity they had displayed in their development of weapons! His eyes were drawn irresistibly to the flaming orbs of the Zara.

She was actually smiling at him, this beautiful, heartless animal, not a smile of derision but one of deliberate allure. He felt the hot blood mount to his temples. A languid arm beckoned him to her side and the amazing creature settled back in her cushions with the drowsy, contented motions of a lazy feline.

"Watch your step!" Tommy hissed.

That warning was unnecessary. Blaine shook his head and backed away from the dais, an instinctive recoiling from a loathsome thing. The Zara saw and understood; and she went again into a black rage. She sat stiffly erect and called rapid orders to her men-at-arms.

The Earth men were surrounded instantly, their arms and legs pinioned by powerful hands, their feeble resistance over-

come by the bronze giants as easily as if they had been children. Helpless and hopeless, they were borne from the room.

This was the end of the story, Blaine thought. Why this Zara woman had not made away with them at once was a mystery. Perhaps they were being reserved for an even more terrible fate than that of the hunchback. They were being carried along a dim-lit passage now, and Tom was cursing his captors in a never-ending stream of invective.

A metal door opened and then clanged shut behind them. They were dumped unceremoniously on metal tables that resembled those of a hospital operating-room on Earth. Woven bands, quickly adjusted by the bronze giants held them fast. Blaine turned his head and saw that Tommy was still struggling against the inevitable. A gag had been placed in his mouth; that was why he had ceased reviling the Zara's servitors.

The room was cluttered with elaborate and complicated mechanisms that Blaine could not recognize in the slightest detail, excepting that there were many banks of slender glass cylinders which bore some resemblance to the vacuum tubes used on the inner planets for radio communication and television. One of the bronze giants, he saw, was bringing a metal cap from which a cable extended to one of the strange machines. This cap was forced down over his head with a none too gentle pressure and he could see no more.

There came a sharp buzz from the machine and a million stinging needles drove into his brain. There was a moment of fleeting visions; strange places he viewed, and strange creatures parading in a fantasmagoria of delirium before his aching eyes. Voices, harsh and guttural, spoke in his drumming ears; voices that were dimly understandable, though uttered in the tongue spoken by Antazzo and the Zara. Then came sudden and merciful unconsciousness.

CHAPTER III

Ilen-dar

When Blaine Carson opened his eyes it was to stare at the blue-white radiance of an illuminated ceiling. He lay on a downy cot and it seemed he had just recovered from a long illness. Weak and sick, he turned his head listlessly to gaze at the ornate embossed designs on a wall of gleaming silvery metal. What place was this? His mind was wool-gathering; dim memories of unspeakable things struggled for mastery over a hazy consciousness. Suddenly then he remembered, and he sat up in his unfamiliar bed, senses acutely alert.

Across the room he saw a figure hunched in a chair; a twisted man-creature who was oddly like someone he had seen. Antazzo! But this one had none of the other's ferocity as he returned Blaine's stare. Rather, there was a look of deep concern in his ugly face. He came immediately to the bedside and looked at Blaine solicitously.

"I see you have recovered," he said. "It is good."

Blaine stared and stared. This creature had spoken in the language of the Zara's subjects, yet he understood his every word! It must be a dream, this impossible thing that had happened. And where was Tom? Abruptly he found that he was talking rapidly in this tongue of an alien race.

"Yes, I've recovered," he said, "and I'm amazed at what I find. How have I acquired this knowledge of your language? Where am I, and where is my friend? Can you enlighten me in these things?"

The other smiled. "I can, Earth man," he replied. "You have been taught our language while you slept. A thought transference process we use for educating the young. You are in the palace of the Zara and your friend is safe in the next room. I may add that you are in high favor with Her Majesty."

The wizened creature lowered his voice on the last words, and his knowing eyes spoke volumes. In favor with that she-devil! Blaine went cold at the thought.

"I want to see my friend," he said shortly.

"Later. My orders are to bring you to the Zara immediately

you are strong enough. And Pegrani obeys orders."

No use to attempt a break now. Blaine was tempted to drive a fist into that ugly countenance and fight his way out of the place. But that would be suicide. He'd wait, get the lay of the land first and then try to dope something out with Tommy.

"All right, Pegrani," he said, "I'm ready to go before this Zara of yours."

As he prepared for the audience, alien thoughts crowded one upon the other in his strangely enlightened mind. With the knowledge of the language had come knowledge of many things relative to the copper-clad world. They'd given him a liberal education. Somehow he knew these stunted creatures like Antazzo and Pegrani were known as Llotta and that, while ruling the sealed-in planet, their kind had originally come from Ganymede, the fifth satellite of Jupiter. Centuries had passed since the inhabitants of Europa and Ganymede had been forced to desert their aging worlds and had settled on Io. During other centuries the widely different peoples had co-operated in constructing the great copper enclosure in order to keep the new world alive and capable of supporting life. Then had come a century of bitter warfare in which the Llotta were victorious. Intense hatred existed between the two races, he knew, and a hazy impression of mechanically imparted knowledge told him that few of the Europans remained alive.

"We are here, Carson," his guide announced, when they stood before the square columns of an enormous portal.

The scene in the throne room was vastly different than when he had first visited it. The Zara sat curled as before, a golden bowl of incense burning at either side of the throne. The men-at-arms were absent and, instead, there were dozens of hand-maidens, white-skinned and seductive as their queen, reclining on luxurious cushions that were arranged in a semicircle before the dais. It was a scene of Oriental splendor. A stage carefully set.

Pegrani knelt and touched his forehead to the floor but Blaine held himself stiffly erect, looking straight into the eyes of the Zara. She smiled and extended her arm in that beckoning gesture.

"You may leave now, Pegrani," she said, without deigning him a glance. "Remain in the corridor until I send for you."

There was a tense silence as the Zara's gaze, ineffably soft-

ened now, held Blaine's. Unconsciously he was drawn to the steps of the dais. Unwillingly, yet inexorably, his lagging footsteps brought him to her side. Cool white fingers touched his arm and he saw that the red flecks in the black of those wide eyes were golden now. Surely there was no harm in this woman. But he remembered Antazzo.

"Carson," she purred, "you are more than welcome to Llotta-nar, the land of my people and the ruling power of Antrid, the body you call Io. The freedom of the realm is yours for as long a time as you wish to remain."

This was too good to be true. "You — you mean," he stammered, "that Antazzo exceeded his authority in his act of piracy — in bringing us here?"

The golden flecks flashed red and a cold note was manifest in the throaty voice. "Antazzo," she replied, "was destroyed for his audacious actions. We needed this k-metal of yours, Carson, and he was sent to Earth to get a quantity of the material. By magnetic directional waves was he sent — we have no spaceships — his body disintegrated by my scientists for transmittal, and the atoms of his beastly form reassembled in their proper relation when he arrived there. But he threatened me when he returned successful. The possession of the k-metal and his knowledge of its powers and uses had gone to his head. He demanded my hand in return for his work; demanded that he be permitted to mount the throne of Llotta-nar as my consort. Therefore I destroyed him." The hard eyes softened anew. "And — and for his abominable treatment of you I destroyed him," she concluded.

Blaine fought off the spell of those gold-flecked eyes; he looked away in sudden panic. This creature was not telling the truth. She was hiding something; a sinister motive lay beneath her smooth speech.

"My friend," he said abruptly: "what of him?"

"For your sake, my Carson," she purred, "he too shall have the freedom of the realm for as long a time as is desired."

The cool fingers crept along his arm, firm and compelling. "Look at me," she whispered.

He thought of the pink gas as his eyes were drawn irresistibly to hers. What he saw in those gold-flecked depths sent a shiver of apprehension chasing down his spine. Savage, devastating

desire mingled with ill-concealed rage at his coldness. This beautiful animal could turn like a flash and rend him limb from limb — and would on the slightest provocation.

A commotion in the corridor caused her to release him and sit bolt upright. Temporarily relieved, Blaine wheeled to face the portal. Tommy had broken loose! He heard his strident voice, berating an unseen antagonist in the tongue of the Llotta.

Then they were in the room, Tommy struggling and arguing vociferously with one of the green-bronze guards. The hand-maidens had deserted their cushions and were milling about in affrighted confusion. The Zara's sibilant exclamation startled him into looking at her once more. The same cold fury that had greeted Antazzo glinted icy-hard in that grimly beautiful face. It was all over for poor Tommy.

But the Zara reached upward and stroked a transparent rod that dangled above the throne, something he had not noticed before. A screaming vibrant note smote the heavy air, a pulsation that beat at the ear drums with painful intensity. Silence fell as the awesome sound died away and echoed faintly from the huge columns that supported the arched ceiling. Tommy cooled off when he saw that Blaine was unharmed.

"Drekan!" The Zara's voice was a whiplash as she addressed the guard. "You will leave my presence and report to your overman for punishment. Never again molest the Earth men. Begone!"

Again this amazing woman curled in her cushions and again she purred. Tommy watched in open mouthed astonishment as she smiled guilelessly on his friend.

"You may leave me now, my Carson," she cooed. "Farley is free to accompany you. Pegrani will guide you and inform you regarding our customs and our people. You will learn much. And then you shall return to Zara Clyone."

Blaine had fully expected that Tommy would die a horrible death before his eyes, and in his sudden relief bent low and kissed the cold white hand of the Zara. A foolish thing to do! She purred and snuggled into the cushions like the feline she was — a dangerous animal; claws drawn in now but ready to strike out, razor sharp, on a moment's notice.

* * * *

Pegrani led them along the corridor to a lift. The car shot upward with breath-taking speed.

"Say!" Tommy was growling, in English. "What's the big idea? You've got the old girl ga-ga. Trying to vamp her into letting us off easy?"

"Shut up!" Blaine returned, irritated. "I don't know where we stand any more than you do. But we're going to sit tight now and see what happens. No more rough stuff from you, either."

"What! You're going to just stand around and take it — whatever they hand us?"

"Of course not. But the time isn't ripe yet. We'll have to wait till we know what it's all about."

They were outside then, on the palace roof, and Pegrani motioned them to a railed-in runway that circled its edge. High overhead was the shadowy blackness of the copper shell that enclosed the satellite. Huge latticed columns, line upon line of them, stretched off into the distance as far as the eye could follow; enormous white metal supports that carried the immense weight of the covering which retained the dense and humid atmosphere. Myriads of tiny blue-white suns there seemed to be, stretching off between the columns, carried on thick cables and radiating the artificial daylight of the interior. Hot, damp odors wafted across the roof, the odors of decayed vegetation.

Most amazing of all, were the dwellings. In orderly rows like the columns, they were flat topped cylindrical things that reminded Blaine of nothing so much as the tanks of an oil refinery back home. And the space between was overgrown with dense tropical vegetation, tangled and matted and shooting transparent tubular stems up to a height of a hundred feet or more where they sprouted great spherical growths that looked like enormous sponges. Of a sickly, pale green hue, these growths overran everything; climbed the columns and were lost in the shadows above the multitude of lights. The big sponge-like blossoms expanded and contracted rhythmically. Breathing, they were, like living things. Specially cultivated plant life to assist in maintaining the oxygen supply balance by decomposition of carbon dioxide. A marvelous artificial world!

"The streets and moving ways are in tunnels beneath the soil," Pegrani was explaining. "What lies before you is the city of

Ilen-dar, capital city of the empire, and like all other cities of Antrid, it is self-sustaining. The vegetation is inedible, all of our food is synthetic and highly concentrated. You were fed by intravenous injection while under the influence of the language machines. Our heat and power is obtained from the internal fires of Antrid, and, alas, these are being exhausted with great rapidity. Our shortage of power is becoming acute, and again our peoples are facing extinction."

That explained their need for the k-metal. It came to Blaine in a flash that Antrid was in sore straits and that this expedition to Earth had more back of it than had been revealed. Even with the supply of k-metal Antazzo had stolen, they could not carry on forever.

A screaming object went hurtling through the blackness over their heads. Something, a vehicle of enormous size with rows of lighted ports on the under side, that roared its way under the roof of copper and was gone in an instant.

"One of our monorail cars," Pegrani told them: "a complete system interconnects all cities and divisions. They are capable of circling the globe in a day of your time."

Their familiarity with conditions on Earth was astonishing. Probably Antazzo was but one of many spies who had been sent to the inner planets. Pegrani discussed the speed in their own terms.

Someone had crept up behind them; a slight, olive-skinned youth who touched Blaine softly on the shoulder. Pegrani did not see. He was pointing into the distance and expounding on the merits of the monorail system. The youth touched a finger to his lips to enjoin silence, and thrust a crumpled ball of metal foil into Blaine's hand before the pilot realized his intention. A message, undoubtedly!

Some instinct, or some slight sound, warned Pegrani and he turned on his heel just as the slender lad was slinking away. Black rage contorted his features and Blaine saw him make a quick motion toward the inner folds of his jacket.

"Pegrani!" he shouted as he saw a glint of steel. "Don't!"

But it was too late and the Llott paid him no attention, anyway. One of those wicked ray pistols sent forth its crackling blue flame and the youth stood there, bathed in the eery blue light; dazzling blasts of exploding atoms were seen within the

flare. Then there was the nothingness into which Wahoney and Kelly had gone.

Blaine shouted horrified and angry protest and Tommy rushed in to mix it with their guide. But the glowing ray pistol waved them back. Other guards — the big green-bronze ones — were running in their direction.

"The message!" Pegrani snapped. "Give it to me."

Quick as a flash Blaine crumpled the foil more tightly. A hard little pellet now, he tossed it over the rail far into the matted vegetation below. One might as well hunt for a needle in a haystack as for that tiny ball. But Pegrani would not forget; he'd report to the Zara. They were in for it now.

CHAPTER IV

Before the Council

Pegrani lost no time in reporting the incident to the Zara. The Earth men were hustled to the throne room of the palace where the leopard woman sat in conference with her advisers. An ominous silence greeted their entrance. Ugly faces leered at them from the long table.

"What is it, Pegrani?" The Zara's chalky face went whiter still.

"The Rulans, Your Majesty. They have endeavored to communicate with the prisoners."

"Did they succeed?" Clyone's voice was terrible in its fury.

"They did not. I destroyed the messenger, and the message itself was lost in the jungle where Carson flung it."

The Zara shot a fleeting glance in Blaine's direction and permitted herself the ghost of a smile. "It is well," she breathed. "But it must not happen again. Have Tiedor brought to me."

Pegrani hurried off to do her bidding and Blaine turned uncertainly to follow.

"You will remain, Carson — you and Farley." The incisive voice of the leopard woman halted him in his tracks.

Tiedor was chief of the Rulans, it developed. There was but a handful of them in the realm and they were the last survivors of the civilization of Europa; descendants of those original brave souls who had settled on Io as a last resort in the effort to perpetuate their kind.

He was a magnificent creature, this Tiedor, tall and straight in his muscular leanness and with wide-set gray eyes in the face of a Greek god. Olive-skinned like the messenger, he was, and with the high forehead of an intellectual. He swept the assemblage with a haughty gaze when he faced the Zara.

"Tiedor," she snarled, "it has come to my ears that a Rulan lad carried a message to one of my guests from Earth. What means this?"

"I know nothing about it, Your Majesty." Tiedor gazed into the wicked eyes, unafraid.

"You lie! There is some treasonable scheme in which you

had hoped to enlist their help. You will tell me the entire story, here before the council."

"There is nothing to tell."

"You will confess or I shall destroy every Rulan in the Tritu Nogaru." The Zara's words were clipped short with deadly emphasis.

Tiedor paled and his lips tightened in a grim line, but he stood his ground. "I have nothing to confess," he said.

With a whistling indrawn breath, the leopard woman threw back her head and motioned to one of the green-bronze giants who guarded the entrance. There was a nervous stir around the council table.

At her command the guard drew back a heavy drape that hid an embrasure in the far wall. There, on a stubby pedestal, was revealed a gleaming sphere of crystal, a huge polished ball that shimmered a ghastly green against a background of jet.

Slowly in its depths a milky cloud took shape, swirling and pulsating like a living thing. Then it flashed into dazzling brilliance and the globe cleared to startling transparency. It was as if it did not exist. Rather they looked through an opening in the cosmos that carried their gaze to another and distant point. It was a large open space that was revealed to their eyes; a sort of public square where many of the olive-skinned Rulans were coming and going to and from the entrances of the circular tank-like structures that surrounded the area. They were greeting one another in solemn fashion as they passed and watching furtively the green-bronze guards who were everywhere. The sound of their low voiced conversations came clear and distinct from the depths of the crystal sphere.

"Your choice, Tiedor," the Zara hissed.

"There is nothing — nothing, I tell you!" The Rulan chief's voice was panicky now.

Clyone's snarling command was carried to those guards out there in the Tritu Nogaru by some magic of the crystal sphere. As one man they snapped to attention. With deadly accuracy they released the energy of their ray pistols. It was a shambles, that square of the Tritu Nogaru; a slaughter house. Agonized screams of the doomed Rulans rent the air of the council chamber. They organized hastily and rushed again and again into the crackling blue flame of the disintegrating blasts of the guards' fire. It was

hopeless: unarmed and unprotected, they were at the mercy of Clyone's minions.

Sick and trembling, Blaine cried out against the massacre. He was seized instantly by two of the green-bronze guards who had been watching his every move. Tommy, too, was in their clutches once more, fighting valiantly but without avail. The sphere went blank and silent, and the drape was returned to its place. Still muttering disapproval, the members of the council gazed at their queen in alarm. There was no telling what this vile creature might do.

"The slaughter continues. Tiedor," she gloated. "Soon your handful of followers will be no more. And good riddance."

Swaying drunkenly, eyes glazed with the horror of the thing. Tiedor went raving mad. In one wild leap he was upon her, his fingers sinking into the white flesh of her throat. Woman or no woman, he'd have her life.

But it was not to be. A quick move of jeweled fingers was followed by a crashing report. Tiedor staggered and drew back, spinning on his heel to face them all with distended, pain-crazed eyes. Astonishment was there, and horror, but the fire of undying courage remained. His olive skin turned suddenly purple, then black from the poisoned dart that had exploded in his entrails. He collapsed in a still heap at the feet of the Zara.

She stood there a moment in the awful silence, caressing her bruised throat with fluttering fingers. She had faced death for one horrid instant and was obviously shaken.

Then she recovered and flew into a rage. "Out of my sight, all of you!" she screamed. "Out, I say! The Earth men are to be freed and Pegrani will conduct them to their quarters. Go now!"

The councillors made haste to comply, jostling one another in their anxiety to jam through the doorway. Blaine found himself released. He took one step toward Clyone, murderous hatred in his heart. But he recoiled from the expression in those red-flecked eyes; they softened instantly and looked into his very soul, saw through and beyond him into some far place where relief and happiness might be attained. And then, suddenly, they were swimming in tears. The Zara dropped into a seat and buried her sleek coiffured head in outstretched arms, her shoulders shaking with sobs.

An incomprehensible anomaly, this queen of the Llotta; a

strange mixture of cruelty and tenderness, of cold hatred and the longing for love. A dual personality hers, susceptible to the deepest emotion or to utter lack of feeling as the mood might dictate.

Blaine tiptoed softly from the room.

****

They were in the corridor now, and Tommy was blowing off at a great rate. Even Pegrani was stunned and shaken. But Tommy raved.

"Forget it!" Blaine growled. "Where do we go from here?" He couldn't have explained his emotions then, even to himself.

"To our quarters, she said — damn her!" Tom Farley swore in picturesque English. "And we," he wound up his expressive tirade, "are getting in deeper and deeper. We can't do a thing. Why in the devil doesn't she put us out of the way and get it over with? What's she keeping us around for, anyway?"

Blaine was asking himself that very question. Pegrani regarded them with something of understanding in his beady eyes. But he was nervous and apprehensive and broke in on their conversation to urge them into action. The Zara must be obeyed.

The corridor was deserted now and their footsteps echoed hollowly from the bare metal walls. Pegrani was ahead, leading the way, when Blaine was startled by an insistent tap on his shoulder. Another of the Rulans, it was, repeating the gesture of the youth who had been killed on the roof. But this one had no message; he was after something else — telling them in pantomime to make a break for freedom and to follow him.

Blaine caught Tommy's attention. And Pegrani, warned again by that sixth sense of his, turned his head. With a bellow of rage he whirled into action, ray pistol in hand. But Blaine was prepared for him this time. He wasn't going to witness another murder — not now. Flinging Tom Farley aside, he let loose a terrific jab that landed full on Pegrani's mouth. The ray pistol crackled harmlessly, its deadly energy spending itself in searing the metal of the ceiling.

Then he wrenched the weapon from the astonished Llott and was boring in with body punches that quickly had the dwarf gasping for breath. These creatures knew nothing of fighting with their hands except in the fashion of clumsy wrestlers. The thud of hard fists against yielding flesh was a new and terrifying

experience. Pegrani was game, though, and he flailed about with his powerful arms, endeavoring to get his opponent in his grasp. Sidestepping to avoid one of his rushes, Blaine brought up a terrible uppercut that ended flush upon the Llott's jaw. His head snapped back and his knees gave way beneath him. Down he went in a flabby heap. Suddenly ashamed, the young pilot turned to the Rulan.

Tom's eyes were shining. It was easy to see that he felt better about things now.

"I am a friend," the Rulan whispered in the Llott tongue, "sent by one who would have conversation with you. It is of the highest importance, but we must make haste. Will you trust me?"

Blaine saw deep concern and sincerity in the fellow's blue eyes. "What do you say, Tommy?" he asked, looking to his friend for approval.

"I say, let's go. He seems okay to me."

Their new guide was familiar with the passages and especially so with dark and little used stairways that connected the floors of the huge building. They soon reached the roof through a hatch that opened on a small penthouse which was in deep shadow and entirely hidden from the runways where the green-bronze guards paced constantly.

A slender cable dangled before them, and at its lower end they saw a basket-like car which their guide bid them enter. When they had done so, he tugged on the cable, giving a rapid twitching signal. Instantly they were soaring up into the blackness above the lights of Antrid.

The swift journey ended in a tiny enclosed vehicle where another Rulan operated the cable drum which had made the trip possible. The car was unlighted save for the faint glow of a hand lamp, and it was not until the lower door was closed that they were permitted a view of the interior of the strange vehicle and had a good look at the two Rulans.

"Now," the one who had brought them said, "I can explain. I am Tiedus, son of Tiedor. My companion is Dantus, son of Dantor, the greatest scientist in all Antrid. We are taking you to Dantor who has knowledge of the mad plans of the Llotta and is in need of your help in thwarting them. You are willing?"

"Why — why, yes," Blaine stammered, looking deep into the

earnest eyes of Tiedus. "You — you know of the fate of Tiedor?"

"I do." The young Rulan fell silent; then shook his head as if to clear it of unwelcome thoughts. "There are but few of us left, oh Earth man," he said then, "and all expect a like fate sooner or later. But that is beside the point. We have important work to do: work that brooks no delay. We leave now for the Tritu Anu, with your consent."

Tom Farley was examining the machinery of the car with interest. "This one of the monorail cars?" he inquired, when Dantus had seated himself at the controls.

"Indeed not. The Llotta do not even know of the existence of this vehicle. We could not get right of way on the rails, so this gravity car was developed in secrecy. It is provided with variable repulsion energies that can be adjusted to keep it at a fixed distance from the inner surface of the copper shell. Thus it misses cross beams and braces. It is drawn forward by similar energies, or more exactly, by the component of a number of attracting forces. We do not display lights, so are thus comparatively safe from discovery. They'll catch us sooner or later, though, of course." Dantus indulged in a fatalistic shrug of his shoulders as he concluded.

At his manipulation of a number of tiny levers that were set into the control panels like the stops of an organ, the car lurched forward. Silently, swiftly, they sped on through the gloom under the great copper shell.

Through the viewing glass of a periscope arrangement that let no betraying light escape to the outside, they watched the endless lines of illuminating globes slip by beneath them. Weirdly vast and shadowy in the upper reaches, the latticed supporting columns on either side merged into continuous semi-transparent walls as the car gathered speed.

The city of Ilen-dar was left far behind. Patches of jungle flashed by; other cities. And always the endless rows of blue-white lights. There was neither night nor day in the sealed-in world; only the artificial suns that never set. Continuous subjection to the ultra-violet and visible rays of the vast lighting system was necessary to the growth and reproduction of the plant life that was so essential in keeping the atmosphere breathable.

Tommy had forgotten everything save his interest in the mechanism of the car. He and Dantus were fast friends already.

Chin in hand and eyes avoiding the pain of mourning in Tiedus' fixed gaze, Carson lost himself in gloomy meditation. As he thought back over the events of the past few days he could scarcely believe they had actually occurred or that he was sitting here in a mystery car, speeding through the rank atmosphere of an enclosed world a half billion miles from his own. Home seemed incredibly remote and desirable just then, and the future dark and forbidding.

CHAPTER V

The Tritu Anu

Before the car came to a stop Tiedus rummaged in a locker and stretched forth his hands as if carrying something delicate and fragile.

"It will be necessary for you to put this on," he said: "it will be unsafe otherwise."

Blaine stared, mystified. Was this Rulan kidding him? "Put what on?" he asked.

"A thousand pardons. I had forgotten that you do not know. I hold in my hands a cloak, an invisible thing that will hide you from the guards and from the Zara's crystal. Another secret of my father's. Dantor developed it for him only recently."

Blaine felt the texture of the stuff then; crumpled it in his fingers as its gossamer-like weight dropped in loose folds around his body. But there was nothing there: to the eyes. It simply did not exist except to the touch, and he felt no different with it on than he had before.

"Where's Tommy?" he asked suddenly, seeing that Dantus now sat alone at the controls.

Tiedus laughed. "He has been covered in the same manner," he said, "and is safely hidden from sight as are you."

Incredulous, disbelieving, Blaine called out to his friend in a tremulous voice. And Tom Farley's awed response reassured him.

"Keep close to me," Tiedus told him. The car had stopped and he directed them into the basket of the lift. The two Earth men collided violently and, clinging to each other in their ghastly invisibility, laughed crazily for a moment. As far as any observers might know there were only the two Rulans in the basket.

Blaine fingered Pegrani's ray pistol when the cable lowered them swiftly to the roof of a huge steel cylinder that rose, a solitary and unlovely structure, in the midst of the jungle a thousand miles from Ilen-dar. The indicator informed him that seven energy charges still remained in the storage chamber of the little weapon. Its possession brought him a measure of confidence.

Careful scrutiny of the roof had shown it to be deserted, so the basket was brought to rest in a deeply shadowed portion. Immediately they stepped out, and it was sent swiftly aloft by remote control of a portable ether-wave that Dantor produced.

They encountered two of the green-bronze guards in one of the passages below and these challenged the Rulan lads with drawn pistols. The alarm was out! Fortunately Pegrani had not recognized Tiedus or all would have been lost. But the Zara was watching every Rulan community and had instructed her guards to take the Earth men into custody at all costs. Those remarkable cloaks were all that saved them. They breathed easier when the guards passed on.

Now they were in a lift, dropping speedily into the depths of the Tritu Anu. When the cage came to rest they were hustled into a maze of winding passageways that led ever downward. A wall of damp stone finally blocked their progress, but at Dantus' touch of a hidden spring a section of the solid rock swung aside to admit them to a concealed room where the lights were bright and where a delegation of Rulans awaited their coming.

With the cloaks of invisibility removed, they were welcomed by Dantor, a tall white-haired Rulan who was startlingly like his son.

They were a solemn lot, these Rulans of the older generation, but they gazed on the Earth men with sympathy and understanding. An entirely different breed from the Llotta.

This room was a secret laboratory, fully equipped for chemical and physical research. Dantor sat before a smaller replica of the Zara's crystal ball as he addressed the visitors.

"No doubt you are puzzled," he began, using the language of the Llotta with an accent that softened its harsh gutturals, "over the calamity that has befallen you. And it is not to be wondered at. But your own danger is as nothing compared with the danger that now threatens our whole solar system. It is to explain that and to ask your cooperation in warding off the holocaust that I have sent for you.

"Since the destruction of the Tritu Nogaru we Rulans number less than one thousand, of whom three hundred are here. The Tritu Anu is foremost of the royal laboratories of Llotta-nar and its work is carried out entirely by our people. It is only on account of our superior accomplishments in science that the

Llotta have allowed us to exist for so long a time, and, in this connection, I might say that the Zara has been taken severely to task for her wanton massacre of the Rulans of the Tritu Nogaru. But that is neither here nor there; it is merely a sidelight I am giving you.

"The important thing is this k-metal of yours and its relation to the plans of the Llotta. Antrid, as you know, is a dying world; coming rapidly to the end of its resources. And, as our ancestors did before us, the Llotta have been casting their eyes about for a new home. The inner planets beckoned, especially your Earth, but it was manifestly impossible to reach them as there is insufficient fuel in all Antrid to provide for the voyage of even one space ship. Then, with the long range searching rays of the crystal ball television and sound reproducers, they discovered the use of this k-metal. The sending of Antazzo to your Earth followed.

"The rest you know insofar as his activities are concerned, but what you do not know is this: The Llotta have constructed a huge steel tube that is set deep into the crust of Antrid; an enormous rocket-tube if you please, like one of those on your space ship. They plan to use the energy of this supply of k-metal in setting up tremendous streams of electronic discharges from the great tube and thus to swing the satellite from its natural orbit. They would send this entire world hurtling through space toward the inner planets, and, by proper control of the rocket discharges, bring it close to your Earth where it would become a secondary satellite at close range. Then they could war on you at their leisure and finally take Earth as their new home. Thus have the Llotta planned."

"What!" Blaine exclaimed. "Why, we'd blast them from the skies before they were started. They haven't a chance."

Dantor nodded gravely. "I am sure of it," he agreed: "I have seen your great guns in the crystal. But they are blind to that possibility. And there are other serious flaws in the plan. The incentive, of course, lies in the certain knowledge that we are using up the internal heat of Antrid so rapidly that less than a century of life now remains to its peoples. Our power is produced by admitting water to the interior through myriads of tubes that serve the double purpose of introducing the water and conveying the generated steam back to the surface, where it

produces electricity by driving great turbine generators. This electricity is distributed by charging the copper shell and the ground beneath at high frequency; it is collected from the air between by the heaters and various machines that use it. But the shortage is ever more serious and Antrid is cooling off. Thus the need for the k-metal and thus the sending of Antazzo. And now for the flaws:

"The Zara, in killing Antazzo, frustrated her own plans, as he alone, of all her people, knew how to use this marvelous energy producer. Realizing this, she set about to make friends with you two in the hope that the information might be obtained from you. That was a great mistake and raised an unexpected obstacle."

"Well, I'll be damned!" Blaine exploded. "No wonder she tried her wiles on me. Tried to make a sucker out of me, didn't she?"

Dantor smiled knowingly. "More about Clyone later," he said. "Actually she is enamoured of you, Carson, and besides she is not really responsible for the mad plan herself. But that tale can wait.

"The basic and most serious flaw in the plan is this: It can not possibly succeed, no matter how successful their attempts. What they do not understand and will not believe when I tell them is that the only result of the mad experiment will be the complete destruction of the solar system, Antrid and themselves included. Complete and horrible annihilation, I say!" Dantor paused and eyed his visitors solemnly.

In his mind's eye, Blaine could not visualize such a thing nor picture the possible explanation. But he saw that Tommy had paled and was clenching his fists. Tommy was more of a scientist; it must be he realized what this enterprise involved.

Dantor was speaking again, in low, intense tones: "What they are refusing to see is that the delicate balance of the solar system will be disturbed if a body as large as Antrid is moved a half billion miles sunward. All bodies are kept in their orbits by a nice balance of mass attraction and centrifugal force; if a single one is altered all others are affected. What would happen is easy to calculate. First off, when Antrid approached the inner planets all bodies in the system would change their paths and the altered forces would cause severe earthquakes, tidal waves and other

natural disturbances of disastrous extent.

"These would increase in violence as Antrid drew nearer to the sun, and, if she finally took up her position as a new satellite of the Earth, the entire solar system would be in chaos. By this time, even if life still remained on Earth, it would quickly become extinct, for the vastly increased tidal forces on that body would flood the land to the peaks of the highest mountains. Earth would draw in closer to the sun due to loss of velocity and increased mass of the Earth-moon system. Tremendous new forces would rend asunder the Earth, its moon, and Antrid. Venus and Mars, following suit as the forces equalized, we would have a dead universe."

Tommy believed him. That was apparent from his furrowed brow and grim set jaw. "I'll never give 'em the secret of the k-metal," he grated. "Nor will Carson; I'll gamble on that. We'll die here before they'll get it out of us."

Blaine seconded his remarks fervently. Then, turning to the Rulan scientist, "Perhaps," he suggested, "we might remain in hiding here for an indefinite period. Perhaps even we might contrive a way of getting to the store of k-metal and regaining possession of it. They'd be licked for sure then."

Dantor beamed. "That is exactly why I sent for you," he said. Then sobering anew, he added, "But I fear that would not be the end. They will not give up. Another emissary would be transmitted to duplicate Antazzo's exploit on Earth and in five of your years the danger would again be faced. They would take infinite precaution to prevent a second failure. We must make it forever impossible — now."

"How can we? My God, it's hopeless!" Blaine groaned.

"Nothing is hopeless, my boy. Consider the plight of the Rulans. No, there is still hope and we will leave you to think it over — if you are willing. It is necessary that we Rulans show our faces above before we arouse the suspicions of the guards."

"Of course we're willing. We'll stay as long as you say — and help." Blaine was intensely earnest and Tommy chimed in with his old time fervor and enthusiasm. But hope of success seemed remote.

A murmur of approval came from the assembled Rulans, and Dantor wiped a trace of moisture from his tired old eyes. "Thank you," he said simply. "This chamber is insulated from

the searching rays of the crystal spheres. You are safe for the present and will be supplied with everything you need. And I shall return shortly to discuss the matter in further detail."

The two Earth men were alone then, in the uncanny silence of the underground retreat, regarding each other with awed comprehension. What patient, hopeless creatures these Rulans were! Knowing they were doomed, and without thought of their own safety, they were bending their every effort to the impossible task of saving the universe from the madness of the Llotta.

"What do you know about that?" Tommy said, after a while.

"It's true, what he said?" Blaine asked. "What would happen to our world, I mean — and to the rest?"

"Not a question of doubt. He's doped it out to a T. Smart guy, this Dantor."

"What do you think? Is there a chance? Think — "

"Hush!" Tommy interrupted him. "Didn't you hear something?"

The silence was ghastly; depressing. Blaine heard distinctly the beating of his own heart.

Then it was there again, that sound — a muffled scream from the other side of the stone door. A woman's scream of desperate entreaty. A shuddering, long-drawn moan, trailing off into deathly silence.

CHAPTER VI

Ulana

Blaine was tugging at the lever he had seen the Rulans use in opening the stone door from the inside. Tommy, less excited, tried to press one of the invisible cloaks into his free hand.

"Here," he begged. "Don't be a damn fool! They'll get you, the devils."

But the great block of stone was swinging already and the young pilot squeezed through and into the passage. He stumbled over the crumpled figure of a young girl and into the arms of one of the green-bronze guards.

Recovering instantly, he prodded the big fellow's ribs with the ray pistol. "Stick 'em up!" he snarled. Then, realizing the words were meaningless to the other, he said, "Raise your hands — above your head! That's right. Stand still now, or I'll use the ray."

The guard, his face ghastly in the dim light, obeyed. But his wary eyes never left Blaine's for an instant.

A short way down the hall was the body of a young Rulan. Blaine shuddered as he saw it was headless. The ray had nearly missed that time, its energy spent before complete disintegration was effected. The girl lay still at his feet. With quick fingers he frisked the guard, finding his ray pistol and one gas grenade. What was he to do with the big fellow? He ought to let him have it, but somehow he couldn't.

Tommy was in the passageway then, invisible. The big guard stifled an amazed cry as his husky voice came out of the nothingness. These devils of Earth men! They had worked their evil magic on the Zara: had she not ordered that their lives be spared? And now there was this! His thoughts were written large on the ordinarily expressionless countenance, and Blaine was tempted to laugh at his affrighted dismay.

"Come on, you bonehead," Tommy was saying in English. "Bring the big bum inside. I'll carry the girl. Hurry; there'll be a million of them in a minute."

The girl's huddled figure was raised by unseen hands. Poised in mid-air for a moment, it floated joggily, unsteadily

through the crack of the partly opened stone door. The guard, wide-mouthed and staring, muttered supplication to the war gods of Antrid.

Safely inside the secret chamber, the Earth men made haste to truss up the guard and gag him. He was as tractable as a child under the invisible fingers of Tom Farley, with eyes imploring the evil spirits for mercy. And when Tommy's head appeared, drifting, unsupported by a body; to be followed by arms and shoulders that seemed to materialize from nothingness, the big fellow struggled panic-stricken in his bonds, shaking with superstitious terror.

Blaine straightened the girl's limbs where she lay on a low couch. She was breathing in low shuddering gasps, but a swift examination assured him she had not been harmed. Her beautifully chiseled ivory features were fixed in an expression of nameless dread. A mass of red-gold hair tumbled in confusion about her face and shoulders and when the pilot smoothed this back his heart did a most peculiar flip-flop. Sort of jumped into his throat and stuck there. This Rulan maiden was a vision of feminine loveliness if there ever was one; a dream.

Tommy watched him with a cynical smile, and said with mock contempt, "So you're the guy who swore you'd never tangle up with a femme! Just a month ago, too. Now look: first you get this Zara woman all het up over you, and now this one's got you all het up over her. You make me sick!"

There was no fitting retort. Besides, this thing that had come to him was too serious; too big. He couldn't kid about it — even with Tom. Why, he'd always pictured this very girl in his thoughts; had always dreamed of meeting her some day. And here she was: a living, breathing reality. She was stirring, too, now; breathing easier. Her eyes opened wide; frightened, innocent ones like a child's, blue-gray and fringed with long lashes that raised dewy from the smooth ivory of her cheeks.

"Antius, my brother," she exclaimed, remembering, "where is he? I saw — I thought — and the guard; he wanted to take me — oh!"

Hands fluttering to cover her face, she was sobbing now, and

Blaine raised her in his arms, clumsily attempting to comfort her.

"Your brother," he said gently; "I'm afraid the guard did away with him. He is no more."

"Y-yes. I remember now; I saw." She shuddered and became still, her tousled golden head somehow finding a comfortable hollow beneath Blaine's shoulder.

And then, bravely, she sat erect and faced him. "I — I suppose I shouldn't feel so badly," she said. "We always expect it. But I was so fond of him, and he was the last. I am alone now."

"Not alone," said Blaine; "you have me — us, that is. We are the Earth men, you know. And you are safe here."

"You are Carson?" she inquired.

"Yes, and my friend is Farley. That is how your people address us, but we had rather you call us Blaine and Tommy."

Tom Farley was grinning like an idiot. Didn't he have any more sense? Blaine thought. The girl would think he was making fun of her.

"I am Ulana," she said simply.

The stone door opened silently and Tiedus slipped in, closing it swiftly behind him. He stared at the girl and at the trussed-up figure of the guard.

"So!" he exclaimed; "this is the explanation." He breathed heavily as if he had run a long way, and his face was flushed with excitement.

"Why? What's wrong?" Blaine sensed a calamity.

"The Zara — she must have seen you in the crystal. She is in a murderous rage and has visited her wrath on the Tritu Anu. Even now Dantor is on his way to Ilen-dar in answer to her summons."

"Tiedus! I'm sorry. It is my fault entirely, but — but we heard Ulana cry out."

"You did quite right, Carson. I should have done the same myself. And actually it makes little difference as far as we Rulans are concerned. We had not long to remain in this life, anyway. It is only that your hiding place might be revealed; that our plans to outwit the Llotta will fail."

"You — you think she will make away with Dantor?"

"No; he is too valuable as a scientist. But the guards are awaiting her orders to repeat what happened in the Tritu

Nogaru. She depends on the work of this laboratory a great deal, though it may be she will stay her hand."

He was fussing with the controls of the small crystal as he spoke, and it sprang into life with the peculiar shifting milkiness. Then, clearly, they were looking into the council chamber at Ilen-dar. Clyone was there, pacing the floor. Dantor had just arrived with two of the green-bronze guards. The Zara, though nervous, was curiously calm and polite in her greeting of the aged scientist.

"Dantor," she said, "I want these Earth men."

"I can not produce them, Your Majesty."

"You will not, you mean." Clyone dropped her voice. "For two reasons, Dantor, I must have these Earth men. And they must not be harmed. We need them on account of this k-metal that was brought by Antazzo, whose ugly body I so foolishly destroyed."

"Two reasons, you said, oh Clyone?" Dantor smiled knowingly.

"Yes, two!" said the Zara defiantly. "I love this Carson, if you must know. And it is the only influence for good that ever has come into my life, Dantor. Oh, can't you see? I *must* have them."

Blaine felt the hot blood mount to his temples. Tommy giggled like a moron. And Ulana drew away, ever so slightly, it was true, but still it was a definite withdrawal. Damn this leopard woman, anyway!

"He is not for you, oh Clyone," Dantor was saying, "To people of his world the very thought of such a woman as yourself is repulsive. A murderess he would call you! Their reactions to the taking of human life are entirely different from those of the Llotta. They are — you will pardon my saying it — more like those of the Rulans. The Llotta hold life cheap; they hold it dear. To your people you are not a bad woman; only a foolish one who sometimes, in the heat of passion, upsets their plans by the sudden snuffing out of a life that is valuable to those plans. Do you not see my point? He is different; to him you are the wickedest woman whom he has ever encountered — a monster."

This was strong talk. Blaine drew a quick breath, anticipating another of her black rages and sudden death for poor old Dantor.

But Clyone suddenly was on her knees before the old scien-

tist, pleading with him! Creature of strange caprices! Though humanlike in her emotions when in her softer moods, she was more like the feline to which Blaine had likened her, when those soft moods had passed.

Somewhere overhead, in the chambers of the Tritu Anu, there was the sound of a muffled explosion. Its shock was felt even here in the rock-hewn secret apartment. Tiedus went white. Quickly he manipulated the controls of the crystal sphere.

"It can't be," he exclaimed. "The guards would not disobey her, and she has ordered no action."

Swiftly, then, the searching ray of the apparatus swung back to the Tritu Anu itself, boring into the vast structure above them. One of the chemical laboratories was completely wrecked; maimed and dying Rulans were everywhere in the ruins. And those who staggered to their feet were shot down by the green-bronze guards who stood at the doorway.

Then, floor after floor was revealed in the all-seeing crystal. Everywhere it was the same. Merciless, cold-blooded destruction of the Rulan scientists, the most valuable of all in the Llott scheme of things. The Earth men were speechless with horror. Ulana once more buried her head in Carson's shoulder, moaning helplessly.

The scene shifted again to the council chamber of the palace in Ilen-dar. The Zara had not risen from her knees; she was still pleading with Dantor. She knew nothing of the massacre.

"Ianito!" Tiedus gasped. "It must be he."

And once more the view was changed. They were in the huge dome through which they had entered this mad world. Near the base of the great telescope a bullet-headed Llott was gazing into the depths of one of the crystal spheres, watching the carnage in the Tritu Anu and shouting his orders to the guards. "Slay, slay, slay!" he yelled. "Not a Rulan shall remain in all Antrid. It is Ianito commanding you, Ianito the Great, master of our destinies, Dictator Supreme. Let not one escape; I command it. Then will come the great day of release; of conquest. A new home, a new world awaits you for the taking."

"It is as I thought," Tiedus groaned: "it is the end. He has taken things in his own hands at last."

The sphere went blank at his touch of a lever. His shoulders drooped and he spread his hands in a gesture of resignation.

"What in the devil!" Tommy exploded. "Can this guy over-rule the Zara? Is he that powerful?"

"He is actual ruler of the world that is Antrid; the power behind the throne. Clyone must do his bidding. He has seen that she is softening and resolved to speed things up himself."

A sudden bedlam could be heard in the corridor outside the stone door. This Ianito had gone the Zara one better. He had located them; probably saw the capture of the guard and the rescue of Ulana on the very spot where his minions now hammered for entrance.

"They will take you!" Tiedus whispered. "There is no doubt as to the orders issued by Ianito. They will take you alive and bring you to him. You will be compelled to yield the secret of the metal that energizes."

"Not on your life! We'll refuse." Blaine was very positive.

Tiedus smiled sadly. "There is the pink gas, you know," he reminded him. "No, Carson, there is but one way. You must go out into the jungle and hide for a time. Dantor will return later; it is certain he will be spared. And he will contrive some way of outwitting them. Come; there is a passage."

Blaine saw the wisdom of the argument. It was their only chance. There was a blast that shook the ground beneath their feet, and a huge section of the stone door was blown into the room. He drew Ulana close with a possessive encircling arm.

They were in a dark narrow passage now, following the whispered voice of Tiedus. It was damp and rankly odorous there in the darkness, and slimy things wriggled over the floor, brushing their ankles clammily. Behind them there was the roar of another explosion and the shouting of angry voices. The guards were in the secret chamber and hot on their trail.

Tiedus was fumbling with something ahead of them where they had halted; something that rattled and clanked and finally came free. A door opened into the deep-shadowed green of the jungle.

"Go now, quickly," he warned them. "Hide yourselves as far in as you dare go. You will be lost, but will later be directed by a mental message from Dantor. I shall advise him from the spirit world. We do that, you know, we Rulans. But I must leave you

now; I must hold back the guards to give you time. Go, friends; farewell."

In his hand Tiedus held the ray pistol they had taken from the captured guard. He would account for a few of the Llotta at least. Blaine reached for him to restrain him; it was unthinkable that this fine lad should sacrifice himself for them. But Tiedus was gone; he had slipped away into the black depths of the passageway.

"Come on, snap into it!" Tommy grated, his voice brittle with suppressed emotion. "The kid's right; let's go." He pushed his way into the matted growth of the jungle.

Holding Ulana close and not daring to look into her eyes lest he should see what he knew was there, Blaine followed his friend. The mysterious depths of the pale green forest closed in about them.

CHAPTER VII

In the Jungle

They had progressed not more than twenty paces into the dense undergrowth when the gleaming wall of the Tritu Anu was entirely hidden from view. The artificial sunlight seeped through the mass of vegetation overhead, a ghostly green twilight that made death masks of their faces. But of the lights themselves, of the great latticed columns, of the enormous sponge-like blossoms of the upper surface of the jungle sea, nothing could be seen. They were deep in a tangled maze of translucent flora that was like nothing so much as a forest of giant seaweed transplanted from its natural element. The moss-like carpet beneath their feet was slushy wet and condensed moisture rained steadily from the matted fronds and tendrils above. The air they breathed was hot and stifling; laden with rank odors and curling mists that assailed throat and head passages with choking effect.

Weird whisperings there were from above and all about them. It seemed almost that the uncanny, weaving green things were alive and voicing indignant protest over the intrusion of the three humans.

Ankle deep in the rain-soaked moss, their clothing drenched and steaming, they pressed ever deeper into the tangle. All sense of direction was lost.

"Guess we'd better rest now," said Blaine, seeing that Ulana was gasping from her exertions, "They'll never trail us here."

"How about this crystal thing — the searching ray?" Tommy ventured.

"It can not follow us," the girl explained, "Certain juices of the plants provide an insulator against the ray. In fact, it was an extract of these that was used in protecting the underground laboratory we just left. We are safe now and I am very tired."

So that was the reason Tiedus had been so certain they would be safe in the jungle! Blaine had wondered about that searching ray, and now Ulana's statement had stilled his doubts. Poor kid — she was all in! Her shoulders drooped and she leaned on his arm for support. His conscience troubled him for

having forced the pace in the difficult footing. They need not have come so far in.

Aglint of light through the close packed stems caught his eye; something phosphorescent it was, shining there in the green twilight. A giant mushroom! Towering seven feet from the ground, the great umbrella-like top was aglow with sulphurous light on its under side. And, beneath its ten foot spread, the mossy carpet was dry. An ideal shelter. Here Ulana might find the rest she so sorely needed, and in comparative comfort.

She curled up beside the huge stem and, half buried in warm, dry moss, immediately fell asleep. The Earth men sat gazing solemnly at each other; speechless. In the dim distance the roar of a monorail car rose faintly at first, then grew louder and louder, only to fade away once more into the whispering silence. A steady patter of jungle rain drummed on the mushroom top.

"God!" Tommy muttered, after a while. "I'd give my right eye for a cigarette."

"Me too." Blaine was hugging his knees, nodding drowsily. "A nice rare steak with mushroom sauce wouldn't go so bad, either," he drawled.

"Aw, have a heart. I'm so sick of these vitamin pills of theirs I never want to see one again."

"Yeah, but they're better than nothing. We haven't any of those even."

"Say!" Tommy jumped to his feet in sudden remembrance. "I saw a bush, back there about fifty feet, with bunches of big red berries on it. Like grapes, they looked. May be good to eat."

"Sure, they *may* be. And then again they may be poison. We can't take any chances like that. Leave 'em alone."

Tommy growled unintelligibly and fell to walking around their shelter with nervous strides, keeping just within the dry area and glaring savagely into the steaming jungle. Blaine smiled grimly. Nerves! Tommy always was like that; always had to be on the go and doing something. His own nerves were jumpy to-day. They were in hot water this time, for sure. Had to keep on though; they were still alive, or at least half alive; and the solar system was intact as yet. If only Tom Farley would quit his infernal tramping!

"Cut it out!" Blaine snapped peevishly. "You'll have us both

bughouse. Can't you sit down and take it easy?"

Tommy stopped in his tracks. "Sorry, Blaine," he said. But he remained standing, staring off into the jungle. Then, suddenly he exclaimed, "Say, I'm going for some of those grapes, or whatever they are. I'll bring a mess of them back and we can wait till Ulana wakes up. She'll know whether they're poison or not."

"Oh, go ahead. But don't get yourself lost. Yell out if you can't find us and I'll answer."

"Okay. Don't worry about me." And in three steps Tommy was swallowed up in the undergrowth.

Blaine stole a glance at the girl and something caught at his throat. God, she was beautiful! There must be some way of getting her out of this mess. Dantor, perhaps, might show the way. He ought to be sending that message soon — a mental one, Tiedus said. Poor kid, Tiedus; gone to the happy hunting grounds now, no question of that. And he intended to advise Dantor from the spirit world. As simple as that, it was. They were game, these Rulans. Fatalists, though, and resigned to the inevitable; hopeless. But a wonderful people in a rotten world.

Soon he felt his head droop and in a moment he began to doze.

When he awoke it was to the touch of Ulana's soft fingers on his arm. "We are alone?" she asked.

"Lord!" he exclaimed, rising stiffly and rubbing the sleep from his eyes. "How long have I napped? I shouldn't have."

A swift look around the small clearing disclosed the fact that Tommy was missing. He shouldn't have let him go. A sudden panic gripped him.

"Tommy! Tommy!" he called out.

There was not even an echo in reply. Only the whispering of the jungle overhead and all around them. His friend was gone.

"Ulana," he said, his voice trembling, "we *are* alone. Farley is lost; swallowed up in this terrible forest."

And then, suddenly, she was in his arms. Those wondrous blue eyes, swimming in tears, looked into his own. Soft red lips, upturned, met his lips; clung there.

"I am sorry, my Carson," she said softly, when he had released her: "sorry that your good friend is lost. But perhaps," more brightly — "he has but strayed away. When the mental

message comes you will be reunited. He will hear it as well as you."

Blaine shook his head. In his own heart he knew he would never see Tommy again. He had wandered too close to the Tritu Anu and had been overpowered by the green-bronze guards. Their ray pistols — he shuddered at the thought.

"I have *you* now, my Carson," the girl was saying. "Only you."

In a daze of pain and happiness intermingled, he knew he was holding her close, drawing her fiercely to him. And then, raising dull eyes to stare over the precious head and into the jungle that hid his friend, he froze with horror.

A flat serpent head with wide slavering mouth and beady eyes swayed there directly behind her. Pendant, it was, on a scaly and slimy length of undulating body that coiled high above in the matted growths of the jungle. As he watched, rooted to the spot, the great head drew back and poised, vibrating, ready to strike.

In one quick movement he flung the girl aside and whipped out the ray pistol he had taken from Pegrani. He pressed the release and a whirring sound came from the little weapon. But no crackling blue flame sprang forth to blast this creature into nothingness. Jumping aside, he was thrown to the ground by its lashing body as the great snake struck and missed.

But the pistol was useless. Short circuited by moisture, no doubt. He crouched there, calling huskily to Ulana. She must run for it; force her way into the thick undergrowth where the thing could not reach her. She lay there, helpless with terror. Then, in a flash, she was on her feet dashing to his side. God, the huge head was poised there again! Pulsating! The glittering avid eyes upon them!

Instinctively Blaine raised the pistol just as the head darted downward. The release clicked home. And, wonder of wonders, the blue flame crackled spitefully. Exploding atoms, dazzling in the green twilight. Mighty thrashings of the huge coils high up in the tangled foliage. Crashing and tearing of great stems and rope-like tendrils. But the enormous body was headless; a dead thing in the throes of its final reflexes. Only the one charge had been spoiled; the little pistol had served them well.

He drew Ulana into the thickest of the undergrowth for pro-

tection against the tremendous lashing thing that crashed into the small clearing where the giant mushroom grew. Their shelter was destroyed. He must find another; he must be forever on guard over this girl whose hand clung so confidently to his own as they wedged their way into the thicket.

"Carson! Ulana!" A familiar voice rose above the whisperings of the jungle. A voice familiar, yet unreal; supernatural; a calm, commanding one that did not sound but echoed only in the consciousness.

"Hark!" Ulana gripped his hand more tightly. "Did you hear? It is Dantor. The message Tiedus promised."

In awed silence they waited. A tiny ball of orange fire flamed suddenly in the depths of the rushes directly before them. A sign!

"Ah, you are there!" the voice broke in. "I have your mental reactions. You will follow the orange beacon to the Tritu Anu where I await your coming. Be of good cheer, my children."

What magic was this? The science of the Rulans was beyond the comprehension of the Earth man. Here was telepathy in its most perfect form. Communications from the spirit plane; the orange flame — it was all so utterly fantastic that Blaine had to look earnestly at the girl to assure himself it was not a dream. She smiled confidently.

And the orange flame was moving off into the undergrowth. They must follow its beckoning, flickering light.

It was a nightmare, that journey back through the jungle to the Tritu Anu. Dantor must be in a fearful hurry, for the orange flame moved swiftly. If they stopped a moment to rest it danced there impatiently, then receded into the green shadows until they were forced to follow for fear of losing it. Ulana's light robe was torn and sodden with moisture. The perfectly rounded ivory shoulders, bare now, were scratched and bleeding from contact with thorny protuberances that covered some of the lighter reed-like stems.

But the brave girl was uncomplaining. She clung doggedly to the Earth man's hand when they were able to walk erect: followed swiftly and unquestioningly when they were compelled to crawl or wriggle through an almost impenetrable thicket.

Once she cried out in alarm and Blaine turned back to see that the wiry tendrils of a spiny, globular plant had wound themselves around her slim body and held her fast. As he grasped her

hand to draw her away, others of the tendrils curled about his wrist and he too was imprisoned. They burned the flesh, those writhing things, and tugged mightily. Ulana screamed with the pain of the many that held her in their tightening grasp.

It was alive, this thing that grew there, a huge ball with a thousand stinging tentacles. A carnivorous plant. Even as the realization flashed across his mind he saw that the spiny sphere was opening. Split vertically, the two halves fell apart to disclose the steaming interior whose walls were lined with sharp dagger-like projections a foot in length. And the wiry tendrils were drawing them in!

Almost insane with horror, Blaine released the disintegrating energy of the weapon he still carried in his free hand. Twice he pressed its release and twice the searing blue flame spurted from the glass tube that was its muzzle. Only a few charges remained now in the marvelous weapon but once more it had served then well. The open-mouthed plant monster vanished with the clearing of the blue vapor and the ensnaring tendrils relaxed, falling from their bodies like so many loosened cords. Blaine caught the swooning girl in his arms.

Half carrying her, he struggled on after the orange flare. The base of one of the latticed supporting columns loomed vast in the eery twilight gloom, and he leaned a moment against one of its vine-wrapped members. The girl was exhausted and hung limp in his circling right arm. Still the orange beacon danced on. If only Dantor would ease up a bit. Couldn't he give them a little time?

On and on he staggered, ploughing through the sloppy footing and the dripping clinging greens that were everywhere in his path. Slimy fronds wrapped themselves around them, impeding his progress; clinging as if they too were alive. The whispering silence closed in on them, vast and mysterious. Menacing; awful. . . .

And then he stumbled against a metallic wall. The curved side of the Tritu Anu! His brain cleared and courage returned with a rush. The tiny orange flame danced merrily, leading him along the wall toward the door he knew was there.

Breathing easier now, his pace quickened as Dantor's guiding light slithered along the gleaming wall. Sometimes it was almost hidden from sight by the curvature of the welded plates

and he was forced into a jog trot to keep it in view.

Grimly, tenderly, he clung to the delectable creature whose soft body drooped against him.

The door! The selfsame passage through which they had escaped opened before him. Grateful even for this doubtful protection, he crossed the threshold and trudged wearily along with his precious burden. Blindly trusting in the miraculous powers of Dantor, he followed the orange beacon which now seemed to smile cheerfully as it lighted his way through the winding rock-walled tunnel.

Dazed and spent, he collapsed in the arms of the aged Rulan when he reached the end of the passage.

VIII

Last of the Rulans

Bathed and fed and attired in dry clothing provided by Dantor, the Earth man and Rulan maiden were much refreshed and heartened when, together, they finally faced the aged scientist in the laboratory of the secret apartment. He hadn't allowed them to talk as yet.

Blaine glanced at the ragged opening where the stone door had been blown away. "We are safe from intrusion here?" he asked.

Dantor shrugged expressive shoulders. "The Tritu Anu is empty of life," he said; "a sepulchre. Those of our people who were not completely disintegrated lie blackened corpses in the chambers and corridors overhead. The gas grenades, you know. The guards went to Ianito with Farley and reported you dead: lost in the jungle from which none return."

"Farley!" Blaine shouted. "He is alive?" A wild hope sprang into being, intensified to a certainty as Dantor nodded.

"Why, yes. I thought you knew. They captured him very soon after the escape, but were unable to find you and Ulana. Ianito has mechanized him; he is in a hypnotic state of complete subjection to the Dictator. A quantity of k-metal has been taken to the laboratory at the breech of the great rocket-tube, and Farley now works there with Ianito's crew, initiating them into the mysteries of the metal's uses. Things look very bad."

"Wh-a-at!" Blaine lost his elation over the knowledge that his friend was alive. Tommy was doomed, anyway. They all were doomed. "Why did you bring us back?" he asked, turning away. Blaine felt it was better to have died in the jungle than to face this certainty of lingering torture. Ianito had triumphed; the universe was fated for utter annihilation and Ulana would suffer for weeks, perhaps months, before the final swift dissolution.

Understanding, Dantor smiled gravely. "My boy," he said, "we still live, and while we live there is hope. That is the reason I brought you back. Tiedus' message came to me as his spirit left the body and I made haste to come here as soon as the Zara released me and I knew the coast was clear."

"What hope can there be?" Appalled by the enormity of the disaster that threatened the solar system, certain of the ultimate fate that would be meted out to Tom Farley, and convinced of their own helplessness, Blaine was gloomily unenthusiastic.

"That remains to be seen, Carson. I confess it seems impossible of remedy, but the situation must be faced and studied carefully. Insignificant as we are in the vastness of the cosmos, we may yet prove to be the ones to circumvent the mad plans of the Llotta and prevent the catastrophe which is inevitable if they succeed. We must not give up while we still breathe."

The indomitable spirit of the old scientist glistened in his keen eyes, and he stepped to the controls of the crystal sphere.

"He will not give up, oh Dantor," Ulana exclaimed loyally. "He is with us to the end. Do I speak truth, my Carson?"

Her arm slipped through his and he thrilled anew at her fragrant nearness. Give up? Never! Not with Ulana to fight for. Blaine nodded wordless agreement, silenced by the expression of Dantor's face as the crystal vibrated to a musically throbbing note.

There in the crystal ball was pictured a vast underground workshop somewhat like the one in the great dome through which they had entered the copper-clad world. In place of the telescope there was the butt of a gigantic cannon-like tube that towered and was lost in the shadows of the vaulted chamber. Tom Farley, moving jerkily and staring with glazed unseeing eyes, was working there with a cube of the glittering k-metal. In the open breech block of the tube was a heaped-up cone of dry soil, the material they would disintegrate in producing the blast of electronic forces. Blaine groaned as his friend called for the equivalent of a milligram of radium. Though his voice was listless and his movements uncertain, Tommy knew what he was doing and was giving away the secret, powerless to resist the command Ianito had implanted in his completely subjective mind.

"Ah," Dantor breathed: "progressive annihilation of energy: a thing we never have accomplished. You excite ordinary material such as this dry soil by means of atoms exploded from this k-metal which is in turn excited by ordinary radium that can be used over and over as the primary excitant. Am I correct?"

"You are. There are precise ratios of atomic weights to be

considered, of course, but it looks as if my friend is being extremely accurate in spite of his dazed condition. Man alive! There is enough material there to provide power for the entire planet Venus for a month!"

"And enough to start Antrid from her orbit," Dantor returned. "Enough to send her on her fatal journey sunward?"

"Only for the first acceleration. A vast amount of energy is needed, Carson, since the gravitational attraction of the planet you call Jupiter is enormous. Antrid will be speeded up in its orbit and the increased centrifugal force will cause it to take up a new and larger orbit where the forces will equalize. Several charges will be required in order to free her entirely from the mother body."

"There's time then!" Blaine exclaimed excitedly. "What can we do to put a stop to the thing? Something to counteract this control by Ianito; to cause Tommy to err in his proportions."

"Yes, that would do it — temporarily at least," Dantor agreed, his brow wrinkled in thought; "and there are the invisible cloaks. It is a bare chance if you want to take it. I can show you the way to this underground laboratory, and, in invisibility, you might even be able to change the ratios yourself. Yes, yes, it is a very good idea." The scientist brightened in renewed hope.

"Of course I'll chance it. When do I start?"

Dantor grinned in appreciation and Ulana looked up at him starry-eyed. "I'm going with you," she stated simply.

"Not on your life! There'll be danger. I won't have it!"

"Nevertheless, I'm going. There's another cloak and besides the danger would be greater if I were alone. Where you go I go, and if you die I die with you — gladly." She twined her fingers with his and gazed at him appealingly.

"Dantor! This can't be!" He turned to the scientist for support.

The aged scientist studied the two a little while, and then said quietly, "I'm afraid it is better as she wishes, Carson. I am unable to protect her, my boy, and there is no one else who might give her shelter. We are the last of the Rulans, she and I. The very last."

"Oh-h!" Ulana moaned, pale and distraught. "All — all are gone?"

"All, my dear. In his rage the Dictator destroyed the Tritu

Deanu and the Tritu Raortu when he had finished here. Those were the last settlements remaining, you know. We alone are left behind, Ulana." Dantor bowed his head and the girl sobbed silently.

"Good Heavens!" Blaine Carson was aghast at the revelation. A monstrous deed, this last one of Ianito's. He was a fit master of a world gone mad. A monster in the twisted semblance of human form.

"He will be searching for you, oh Dantor," the girl said with sudden conviction. She had mastered her emotions and was instantly alert to every angle of the situation.

"That is true," said the old man gravely. "For myself I have nothing to fear, of course. Though insanely jealous of my accomplishments, he maintains an armed truce with me. He dares not do otherwise as the Supreme Council is aware of his shortcomings and cognizant of my superior knowledge of science. But there is danger to you two. You must make haste."

A trembling of the ground beneath them lent added emphasis to his final words. A quick glance into the crystal told them that the initial charge was at work in the huge rocket-tube. The laboratory there at its base was in confusion indescribable, the workmen running hither and yon in the effort to escape the terrific heat that radiated from the red hot breech of the tube. They jammed the exits in their anxiety to be anywhere but near this monster source of energy whose pulsating roar drowned out all other sounds in the vast chamber.

Already Antrid was accelerating in velocity. Her vitals were wrenched and twisted, groaning in protest.

"Quick now!" Blaine was adjusting one of the invisible cloaks for Ulana. He'd *have* to take her with him. And a silent prayer for her safety was on his lips.

Invisible now, and hand in hand, they followed Dantor through the deserted passageways to the lift which carried them quickly to the roof. A drumming sound came to their ears as they stood there looking up into the blackness above the blue-white lights of Antrid. Vibrating to the tremendous roar of the rocket-tube, the copper shell emitted a constantly increasing reverberation that was like a long drawn peal of thunder on Earth or Venus. It was awe-inspiring, that sonorous bombilation; deafening.

Dantor was fumbling with the mechanisms of the remote control which Tiedus had used in returning the basket lift to the car that had brought the two Earth men from Ilen-dar. Again and again he returned to his manipulations after peering anxiously upward. But the basket did not respond to the call. They were marooned atop the empty shell of the Tritu Anu!

"Carson! Ulana! Where are you?" the aged scientist shouted above the din, his face a tragic mask, his lips compressed with anxiety and disappointment.

They grasped him to reassure him, each taking a hand. Carson, placing his lips close to the old man's ear, inquired anxiously, "What's the trouble?"

"The car does not respond. Something has happened to the motors, probably on account of the vibration. I can do nothing."

And then, piercingly through the thunderings of the copper shell, a voice broke in — Ianito's voice. "Dantor!" it shrieked. "At last I have found you. I need your help immediately. Wait there for the monorail."

Dantor gripped them tightly to enjoin silence. Ianito had located the scientist with the searching ray and was still watching and listening at his crystal. He seemed not to know that Blaine and Ulana were there.

"Very well, oh Ianito. I shall wait," Dantor shouted.

"It is good. There is important work to be done." Ianito's words trailed off into the maelstrom of sound that swirled about them.

"He's cut off," the scientist yelled. "There is but one chance now. You must come with me, depending on absolute silence and your cloaks to deceive them. It is the only way."

Ulana clung to him there in the terrifying bedlam and Blaine's fingers strayed to the comforting butt of the ray pistol. Whatever happened there were a few charges left; blasts of energy that would serve at least to postpone the end for Ulana. Or, if worse came to worst —

The sudden rush of a monorail car high overhead interrupted his thoughts. "Close to me now!" Dantor shouted; "but have a care lest one of them touch you and discover — "

A cable-hung cage dropped swiftly to the roof and they crowded in beside the scientist. Quickly it whisked them aloft to the higher plane.

In the monorail car Blaine held the girl close, and they trod softly as they dodged the guard at the porthole and stepped into the passenger compartment. Two of Ianito's technical experts were there and a crew of at least a dozen of the green-bronze giants. Unseen by any, the couple tiptoed to the farthest corner of the compartment and took seats in a recessed section.

With a quick jerk and the rising whine of motors, the suspended vehicle started back in the direction of Ilen-dar. In earnest conversation with Ianito's engineers, Dantor affected an air of nonchalance that was artfully disarming. The Llotta suspected nothing as the car continued on its way.

And then there came an ominous grinding sound from underneath the very seat occupied by the invisible fugitives. A puff of dense black smoke followed and Ulana coughed spasmodically, uncontrollably. They were coming now, two of the green-bronze ones, to investigate. There was no escape from this narrow space. And — Ulana was gone! She had slipped from his grasp in the coughing fit and he could not find her with his wildly searching hands. Another betraying cough over there. The green-bronze ones were between them. He saw one of them draw back in amazement, then clench his fingers and twist.

The ripping sound of torn material followed and the girl's head and startled face appeared: floating there, unsupported, her body and limbs as yet invisible. But they'd found her; she was lost!

IX

Ianito

Quickly stripping the protecting cloak from her body, the green-bronze one held the struggling girl gingerly but with a grip of iron. His eyes bulged from their sockets, and the other guard staggered backward with hands outstretched as if to ward off an evil spell that might be cast by this supernatural visitant.

Blaine thrust his arm through the folds of his coat, ray pistol in hand. A crazy laugh forced itself to his lips at sight of the detached member, stretched there, tensed, drifting in mid-air. The pistol prodded Ulana's captor viciously.

"Hands off of her!" the voice behind the lone arm was snarling. "Hands off, or I fire!"

The girl slipped to the floor in a heap as the amazed guard loosed his grip. And, in the same instant, the blue flame spurted. He had not intended to press the release; it was useless anyway to battle the entire outfit. But the blood lust was upon him and a savage joy in the destruction of this beast who had dared lay hands on Ulana impelled him to turn on the other. Blindly he swung, clubbing the pistol and beating in the ghastly face that wobbled there upon the spineless, superstition-bound body.

Others were coming then, hundreds of them it seemed. The pale face of Dantor appeared for an instant in the background, through the red haze that was blinding him. He only knew he was fighting desperately, viciously, and against impossible odds. The satisfying crunch of his left fist against a leering green-bronze face was followed by an excruciating pain as one of his knuckles was driven back. Hardly knowing he had pressed the release of the ray, he was mildly astonished to see that two of the guards were enveloped in the blue vapor. Scintillant tiny sunbursts within the blue. Two less of those devils! His pistol was empty and he flung it into a grinning face; he saw the blood spurt and the face change shape, crushed beyond human resemblance.

He was down then, gasping for breath against the floor plates. The weight upon him was enormous; crushing. If only they'd quit squirming so . . . and pounding . . . reminded him of

his old football days . . . some scrimmage!

Abruptly came the blankness of insensibility.

Dimly at first, in the painful throbbings of returning conscious-ness, Blaine knew he was in one of the Llott workshops where machines hummed and pounded and where many operatives were busily engaged. A cool hand stroked his aching brow and he opened his eyes. Ulana! They had spared her. Alert on the instant, he was acutely aware of the babbling of voices close at hand. Ianito was there, at the base of the huge telescope, talking with Dantor, his voice raised excitedly. The monorail crew stood by, and he noted with grim satisfaction that several of them were as badly damaged as he could wish.

His gaze returned to the sweet face that bent so near. Weakly he drew the golden head to his breast; held it there a moment, thinking, hoping, planning. Then he sat up on the edge of the low couch on which he had been placed, regarding her anx-iously. Evidently they had not harmed her — as yet.

Ianito had dismissed the green-bronze ones and was ap-proaching the couch. Dantor was with him, lagging a little and pressing a finger to his lips; shaking his head gravely to warn them. They must not speak of the plans made in the Tritu Anu; must not talk.

The Dictator was regarding them now with hard eyes. But it seemed almost that something of admiration or respect, some-thing of human-like emotion was in his cold stare.

"Hah!" he grunted, at last. "These two are in love, Dantor. It is as you explained. It is good, and fits in with my plans to a nicety. I shall spare the life of the Earth man on account of his knowledge of the inner planets; I can use him later. The girl I shall spare for a different reason, and that fits in with my plans as well."

What did he mean by that last crack, the grinning devil? A sinister intent was there, behind his smooth talk. Blaine half rose from his seat in quick anger, but the girl's gentle touch on his arm restrained him. She depended on him now and he'd have to go easy until the proper time came.

"Impetuous, aren't they?" Ianito was saying, "these Earth men. A characteristic that must get them into much trouble,

even in their own world."

Laughing at him, this hell-hound! Blaine gritted his teeth.

The Dictator addressed him directly. "You are a fortunate young man," he drawled sarcastically. "You have slain several of my trusted retainers and by so doing have forfeited your right to life. But Ianito is forgiving. Mechanized, you will be of value to me when the great day comes. And it pleases me that you are so deeply attached to the Rulan maiden; it pleases me greatly."

"Why?" Blaine snapped, a great rage consuming him. Only the pressure of Ulana's fingers held him back. He would have to control his temper or he'd make a mess of things.

"Because, my dear Carson, it will so displease the Zara."

With this cryptic remark he turned on his heel and left them. A number of his technical experts awaited him at the eyepiece of the great telescope.

Dantor whispered swiftly before following him, "Keep up your courage, Carson. A way may yet be found."

The group by the telescope was an excited one. Something had occurred which must be of great moment. It came to Blaine in a flash that the reverberations of the copper shell of Antrid had ceased. The rocket-tube was silent.

"I don't know why we shouldn't be in on this," he said to the girl. "Let's go over there and see what it's all about."

One of the astronomers was reporting to Ianito, referring to a sheet of calculations he held in nervous fingers. "Our orbital velocity has increased greatly," he was saying, "and the new path lies at an average distance of eighty-three erds from the mother planet. According to my figures it will require six more charges to free us from her pull and another to redirect us toward our destination."

Eighty-three erds! Practically a million Earth miles. Already they had swung out to a new orbit between those of Ganymede and Callisto. And what of the effect on the other satellites? Blaine listened carefully as the astronomer continued.

"Perturbations in the movements of the other bodies in our own system are marked, and, in the case of the first satellite, have proved disastrous. It has commenced its inward journey and soon will have fallen into the gaseous envelope of the mother body. But this need occasion us no concern; it is small and there

will be stabilization of the others after the second charge is fired."

Colossal conceit! What amazing ignorance or oversight of natural laws! These Llott scientists could see no farther than their snub noses, or at least no farther than the satellite system of Jupiter. And Ianito was complimenting the astronomer on his good work!

The group broke up now and the Dictator turned to the controls of his crystal sphere. Blaine and Ulana caught the view of the underground laboratory at the base of the great rocket-tube.

All was as it had been when they first saw this chamber. The breech of the huge cannon had cooled and its massive block was open. Tommy was there, fishing the radium capsule from the powdery residue in order that it might be used in exciting the next charge. A mechanical precision marked his every motion.

"It is good," Ianito grunted, flicking a lever that cut off the view. "We are progressing nicely, thanks to the generosity of the Earth beings in providing this k-metal."

His sarcastic grin was infuriating. Dantor cast a warning look in the Earth man's direction. It wouldn't do to lock horns with this self-satisfied despot; at any rate, not now. Blaine's mien was expressionless as he faced him.

The view in the crystal was another familiar one when Ianito made a quick readjustment: the throne room in the palace of the Zara! The Dictator snorted when he saw that Clyone was reclining lazily on her golden couch, submitting graciously to the ministrations of her handmaidens.

"Faithless creature!" he snarled. "Harlot! Parricide! But at last Ianito will have his revenge."

The hate in his voice and in those terrible glass-hard eyes was devastating in its intensity: implacable, relentless. Yet Blaine could not down the exultant feeling that came to him when he saw that this monster could suffer, too.

"What's the matter?" he sneered. "Did she throw you down?" He could have bitten off his tongue as he spoke. Ulana gasped.

And if Ianito had been in a rage before he was a madman now. Despite his contempt of the misshapen creature, Blaine quailed before the murderous glare that answered his rash words. But the Dictator was master of himself, at that; his lips

tightened in a thin line and he held his peace. He actually smiled after a moment, the devil, a smile, though, of evil triumph. He turned once more to the crystal and switched on the sound mechanism.

"Clyone," he called, in velvety voice; "it is Ianito."

She looked up, startled, her chalky face gone whiter still. Her jeweled fingers fluttered to the smooth throat.

"I hear you," she replied shakily. "What do you wish of me."

"Nothing much — this time. I have visitors who request an audience with you, oh Clyone. Can you see them at once?"

"Who — who are they?" Her eyes widened at his insinuating tone.

"An Earth man — Carson — and the Rulan maiden who is to become his mate." Ianito chuckled evilly as he watched her expression.

"Carson?" she whispered, her wild eyes softening, "He — he lives?" Black hatred replaced the wondering joy that had glowed in her face. She was thinking of the statement regarding the Rulan maiden. "Why, yes," she snapped, suddenly very much alert; "I can see them. Send them immediately."

The Dictator chortled as he switched off the power. Dantor paled and looked away. So this was his scheme! He was sending Ulana to certain death at the hands of the leopard woman. Blaine bit his lips until they bled. If only he had one of their ray pistols again. If he had —

Ianito was at his side, whispering. But he couldn't see him; the devil had donned one of Dantor's invisible cloaks. Something hard pressed deep into his ribs.

"I shall be with you," the Dictator told him, "but she will not know. It is necessary, of course, that I watch over you in order that your deportment be suitable to the occasion. The death ray of Antrid is ready in my hands. Proceed, you and the Rulan maid, and see to it that you give her every attention while in the Zara's presence."

Dantor interposed an objection, "But, Ianito, you promised to spare them. I learned to love these two and want no harm to come their way."

"I keep my promise, oh Dantor. Ianito will not harm them."

"But the Zara."

"What Clyone does is none of my concern. Silence, Dantor;

I command it! You will remain here." The voice of the Dictator cut like a knife.

The old Rulan scientist bowed his head and turned away. Good old Dantor! He'd done all in his power to help them. This was the end; not a question of doubt. Blaine Carson drew the Rulan maiden fiercely to him. This Clyone might meet some opposition if she attempted to wreak her spite on Ulana; she *would* meet it. There was no need for Ianito to ask that he pay every attention to the lovely, frightened girl who clung to him so trustingly.

They were in the lift then, dropping swiftly into the palace beneath the great dome that topped Antrid.

"This Clyone," Ulana whispered, "she has great power of enticement, my Carson. I fear for your loss — to me. She will take you from me, and I shall be alone — or dead. Death would be the better."

"Never!" said Blaine huskily. "Never, my dear. She has no power over me; nor will I permit her to bring suffering to you."

Ianito laughed then, an ugly cackle that came out of the unseen.

CHAPTER X

Clyone and Ulana

The Zara received them in the throne room, alone. Blaine hesitated as he crossed the threshold, Ulana's trembling fingers tightly clasped in his own. The quick prod of the invisible ray pistol warned him that Ianito was at his heels.

Clyone uncurled her sinuous, black-sheathed body and rose to her feet as they neared the dais.

"Welcome, oh Carson," she purred. "Clyone has mourned you as dead, but she mourns no longer. A kind fate has returned you."

The gold-flecked eyes were all for him; it was as if she did not see his companion. Blaine fought the spell of her with all that was in him. He did not reply.

"Come to me, Carson," she pleaded, her lashes lowered. "Leave this Rulan girl and come to me."

"Where I go she goes," he replied firmly.

"Very well then," said the Zara meekly, "bring her with you. I would converse with her as with you."

Something new, this was: a gentleness Blaine had never thought the leopard woman could exhibit, even in sham. And her eyes, when she raised them, still were gentle. She extended a white arm and smiled provocatively. If this was a ruse, if she meant harm to the Rulan maid, her acting was superb. And, from what he had seen of the woman previously, he was almost convinced of her sincerity. A nature like hers was incapable of successful dissimulation. Still, he was suspicious and he shielded Ulana with his body as they came up to the throne. The Zara studied them in silence for a while. Then she spoke.

"Let me look at you, my dear," she said to the Rulan maiden.

And Ulana, unafraid, faced her boldly. His muscles tensed, Blaine watched every movement of the Zara's straying fingers. But her gaze was direct and kindly; there was no dissembling here. It was not the same Clyone he had previously known.

"You are very beautiful, Ulana," she said softly. "Do you love this Earth man very much?"

"I do, Your Majesty."

"And you, Carson, you love her — very much?"

His answer was wordless. A sudden lump in his throat choked back the vigorous affirmative and he merely nodded, mute, as he enfolded the slight form of Ulana in his arms.

"Carson — are you sure?" Clyone was pleading, her eyes compelling; tender. Ulana drew away from his arms, waiting.

What had come over the leopard woman? She was a creature of mad vagaries, he knew, and yet this was the most convincing mood he had seen. Despite his knowledge of her past; despite his better judgment, he was drawn toward her. A step, and then quick revulsion of feeling. He recoiled and turned swiftly to Ulana.

Clyone saw and understood. Her tender mood was over in a flash and she crouched there, terrible jealous eyes fixed on the Rulan maiden. She extended a white arm with jeweled fingers, pointing. Blaine swung quickly, brushing the arm aside just as that intangible something flashed from her hand. The energy of the black disks! It had missed Ulana by inches, but crashed home — on something!

A scream of terror rang out in the chamber, and there on the floor a dozen paces from the dais the thing that had been Ianito wriggled under the heap of whirring black things that suddenly covered the invisible form. He wriggled and then lay still as the angry buzzing of the black destroyers rose in triumphant, discordant song.

"Ianito!" the Zara exclaimed, thunderstruck. "He was here?"

"He was," Blaine assured her in an awed voice, "invisible, oh Zara, in a cloak contrived by Dantor, the Rulan scientist." Then blind rage overcame him. She had tried to kill Ulana; before his eyes! "You she-devil!" he roared. "I've half a mind to choke the vile life from your tainted body. Damn you! May the heat devils of Mercury burn and sear and shrivel you in everlasting torment."

She cowered as if he had struck her, and, unaccountably, he was ashamed. Cursing her like a schoolboy and using the language of the lower class Venerians!

"Please, Carson, please," she moaned; "do it. Choke me if you will and release me from my torment. I am yours to do with as you please." Throwing back her proud head, she bared her

throat.

Blaine took a step forward, his knees weak beneath him.

"Carson!" It was Ulana, her hand soft on his arm.

He drew the back of his hand across his eyes. This was madness! But was ever a woman so deserving of death? Incomprehensible half-animal creature, she sat there rocking to and fro, waiting.

"No!" he said. "No! Only let us go in peace, Clyone. Your sins be on your own head. Your realization of them is punishment enough."

"Wait!" Controlling herself now, she rose once more, and her face was transfigured. Almost it seemed that she was happy. "Wait!" she repeated. "You are free to go when I have finished, but first Clyone wishes to bid you farewell."

They faced her in silent wonderment.

"Ianito is gone," she continued, "and the Llotta are helpless without him, unless I take over their leadership in fact. He was my master, I admit. But Clyone is able to carry on with the plans he conceived; able, but no longer willing. Clyone is abdicating. It but remains for you, Carson, to put a stop to this thing they are doing down there at the great rocket-tube. You can do it, I am certain. Go now; and think not too badly of Clyone when you have gone. Farewell."

With a quick motion she raised her fingers to her lips, then tossed a small vial crashing to the floor.

"Carson — she has taken something," Ulana stifled a hysterical sob as she spoke. "Go to her. It is the least you can do."

Blaine caught the leopard woman in his arms and lowered her gently to the luxurious cushions of the throne she had occupied for so long a time, a queen in name only. Already the gold-flecked eyes were glazing and they begged him piteously.

"Kiss me." Her lips formed the words, but no sound came.

Ulana was there, on her knees and crying. "Carson, you must," she urged him.

The spirit of Clyone, with its great burden of evil and some little of good, left the beautiful body as the Earth man pressed his lips to hers. An unwonted smile, placid and content, wreathed the still features.

The Zara was no more.

Stunned and shaken by what they had seen, they hurried from the chamber of death. Blaine located the lift and they were quickly carried to the laboratory.

Dantor was there, working with the astronomers, and Blaine drew him aside, whispering the story in his ear in swift disjointed sentences. The aged scientist could scarcely credit his senses.

The thrumming of the copper shell to the energy of the second rocket-tube charge came but faintly to their ears in this place, since the vacuum of outer space surrounded the great domed structure. But the vibration and quakings of the satellite were transmitted to the floorplates on which they stood. They knew that Antrid was swinging ever outward from the mother planet.

"You must do it alone," Dantor was saying; "you and Ulana. I have no control over these Llotta. I am here only on sufferance of Ianito, and Ianito is no more. But they know it not. These in the dome think he is with you now, cloaked in invisibility. The tale of the cloaks has been broadcast. You are safe for the present and can descend to the base of the rocket with impunity. Ianito's name is the password. And here is a ray pistol, fully charged; two of them. He left them in his desk. Go now, quickly."

"The way — how do we get there?" Blaine's fingers closed lovingly over the butts of the pistols and he thrust them in his pockets.

"Oh yes. The lift — the one that carried you to the palace — its shaft ends deep down beneath the natural surface of Antrid in a tunnel where a moving platform will carry you to your friend. May your God and the gods of ancient Antrid be with you."

Once more they were in the cage of the lift, dropping with breath-taking speed. Down into the bowels of the satellite they sped and it seemed the shaft would never end.

Then they were in the tunnel Dantor had told them about, smooth walls speeding past as the swiftly moving platform carried them on. The great arched chamber opened before them at last and they saw that the workmen were returning to their tasks. The huge breech of the rocket-tube had cooled to a dimly visible red, the second charge having done its work.

Hands in his pockets and walking stiffly as if mechanized,

the Earth man presented himself before the guard at the entrance, Ulana pressed close to his side. He feigned the hypnotic state.

"I-an-i-to," he repeated in jerky syllables, acting the part, "he — sent us — with message — for Farley."

The guard grinned. Even here the story of the Earth man and the Rulan maiden was known. The strange leniency of Ianito in permitting them to remain together was the topic of the day. He waved them through with an indulgent gesture. Ianito knew what he was about, and would have his little joke — later.

Tom Farley was there, waiting with the Llott scientists until the breech block should have cooled sufficiently to permit them to open it and prepare the third charge. A flicker of recognition in his glazed eyes told Blaine he was not altogether gone, but Tommy gave no other outward sign. Perhaps with Ianito no longer alive, the mental control would become ineffective.

They had not long to wait, for the breech was water-jacketed and cooled rapidly. Blaine puttered around with unfamiliar test tubes and retorts, watching for a chance to get a word with Tommy in private. He was almost certain that his friend was recovering. Ulana sat there on a greasy bench, regarding the scene with anxious eyes. She was a brick: game as they made them.

Tommy was beside him then, weighing a heap of the dry soil for the next charge. "Are you all right?" Blaine whispered.

But Tom Farley stared back with not a glimmer of comprehension: He was still a victim of the mechanizing process of the Llotta. With a carefully planned but seemingly careless gesture, Blaine slid back the weight on the scale arm. This charge would be short of the proper ratio of dry soil. He wondered what the effect would be.

One of the Llott scientists came over then with the radium capsule, and Tommy attached it to the clamp that would hold it in contact with the cube of k-metal. The dry soil was shoveled into the breech block by the unsuspecting Llotta and the thing was ready for the placing of the excitant.

The great breech block swung home and a siren shrieked. All work in the laboratory was suspended and the workmen stood around in expectant silence. Blaine found himself worrying as to the possible result of his tampering.

"I saw you!" Tommy hissed then in his ear. "There'll be hell to pay now. We gotta beat it."

Good old Tommy! He'd recovered after all. He, too, had been shamming at the last. Blaine saw they were unobserved and thrust one of the pistols in his hand.

"Now!" his friend rasped. "Before they get wise. Grab the girl and we'll make a break for the tunnel entrance: over there."

Ulana took in the situation at a glance and was at his side. They moved swiftly in the direction of the entrance through which they had come.

A terrific roar came from the base of the rocket tube and the Llotta broke into excited screechings. Something different about it this time. There was a terrible menacing note in the jarring thump which preceded the roar. A muffled boom high in the five mile depth of rock strata above them spelled disaster of an unknown and terrifying nature. The breech of the tube was white with heat in an instant of time.

Pandemonium broke loose now and the Earth men were running for the exit to the lift, covering their retreat with brandished ray pistols. Ulana, brave girl, ran alongside, swinging a pinch bar she had picked up, ready to help.

CHAPTER XI

Disaster

The great crystal sphere on the central pedestal was ablaze with the scarlet warning signal of the Supreme Council. A sonorous voice from its depths boomed out above the clamor.

"Kill them! Kill the Earth men," it roared. "The Zara is dead and Ianito has vanished. Denari has mounted the throne, and it is he who commands you. Kill the traitors!"

But the Llotta and the green-bronze guards needed no command from the new ruler of Antrid. These devils from Earth had tampered with the last rocket-tube charge; probably had caused serious damage to the tube itself. They must die.

Only the guards were armed, and the Llotta swarmed so closely in pursuit of the fugitives that it was impossible for them to use their ray pistols. At the great iron gate that now closed the exit stood the guard who had admitted them. Tommy's pistol spurted blue flame and he was enveloped by the destroying energy.

Ulana screamed as a Llott grasped her, wrenching the iron bar from her hands. Blaine covered the intervening distance in a bound and his fist crashed to the fellow's jaw, snapping back his head and lifting him off his feet. He crashed to the floor plates an inert heap and the Earth man recovered the pinch bar.

Pocketing his pistol, he swung the bar with both hands in mighty circles that took terrible toll of the Llotta. They fell back before the onslaught of the infuriated Terrestrial, leaving eight of their number dead or dying with crashed skulls and broken ribs and arms.

"Open the gate, Tommy," he shouted. "Use your pistol on the lock if you have to." A guard was coming at him and he ducked to the floor as the blue flame crackled, singeing the hair from his head and blistering the scalp as it spent its charge in fusing a cross member from one of the steel columns nearby.

He fired from under his prostrate body and the guard thrashed his arms wildly in the blue mist, then stiffened to a sparkling vanishing figure within the dissipating vapor.

A gas grenade burst at his side and Blaine sprang to his feet,

running from the spreading sulphurous cloud. The gate was open and its lock dropped molten metal. Good old Tommy!

The poison gas hid them from their pursuers for the moment and they were through the gate, all three.

"Get back!" Blaine shouted: "the gas!" He held his breath and closed his eyes as he slammed the gate and wedged it with the pinch bar he still carried. That would hold them for a while.

The gas was upon him and his skin flamed scorching hot from the contact. He mustn't breathe: mustn't open his eyes. He groped there in the scalding vapor, blindly. Tommy had him by the wrist then, dragging him away. Ulana was calling somewhere there in the darkness. His lungs were bursting. And then he knew the air was pure, and he exhaled the long pent breath noisily, and inhaled deeply.

Eyes smarting and head reeling, he saw Ulana through a haze of dancing smoke wisps he knew were illusory. She was safe, thank God! They were on the moving platform then, on the return side, and his strength was returning. Narrow escape, he'd had, from that lung-rotting gas. Ulana smiled happily when his vision cleared.

The speeding platform carried them swiftly toward the lift that had brought them down. What if the lift would not operate? This Denari might well have shut off the power or even returned the cage to the upper end of the shaft.

"Boy, oh boy," Tommy was saying, "you sure did gum up the works. Know what happened?"

"Plenty, from the look of things," Blaine smiled grimly.

"I'll say. You cut down the dry soil ratio a third. Not sure of the exact reaction, but the expansion was too rapid. Explosion followed before the air could be driven from the tube. I'll bet the big cannon was wrecked somewhere overhead. Boy, what a blast!"

As if the last sentence were a prophecy, there came a terrific jar that twisted the platform violently from under them. They were thrown headlong and an awe-inspiring rumbling came up from the vitals of Antrid. An earthquake! The tortured satellite could not withstand the strains set up by the tremendous reactive force of the rocket-tube. The lights snuffed out and the platform came to a grinding stop. One of the underground power plants was out of commission and they were trapped here in the

stifling darkness.

"Nice fix we're in now!" Tommy grunted where he had fallen.

Blaine, having located Ulana, was relieved to find that she was unharmed. "Yes," he said slowly; "but there's one thing sure: they can't follow us here unless they walk."

"Why can't we walk?" Ulana asked with forced cheerfulness. "It isn't far now."

"Oh, we can walk all right; we'll have to. And here's hoping we get somewhere." Tommy, at least, was undaunted so far.

It was their only chance now. Blaine held fast to the girl as they felt their way along the smooth tunnel wall, and Tom Farley, behind them there in the darkness, kept up a running fire of small talk that was utterly irrelevant. Nothing could keep that Irishman down.

After what seemed like miles of steady plodding they glimpsed a light ahead. They quickened their pace. It was the open door at the base of the shaft, and the cage of the lift was there, fully lighted and waiting. Denari had not shut off the power after all. But of course! It came to Blaine in a flash; this was a private shaft, used by Ianito in his clandestine visits to the palace of the Zara and for his own use in descending to the sub-surface chamber at the base of the rocket-tube. Denari did not even know it existed.

Strange they had not been followed. Surely the Llotta could have forced that gate back there in a comparatively short time. A mass of falling rock, shaken loose by the temblor that cut off their light and stopped the moving platform, must have closed the tunnel.

They were in the cage now, shooting aloft with smooth acceleration. Tommy fidgeted and paced the floor in the narrow confines like a caged animal.

"Lord, man," he said, after a while, "what I wouldn't give for a cigarette!"

"Is that all you can think of?" Blaine was sarcastic. His own nerves were on edge. They were nearing the upper end of the shaft. "Try to do a little thinking about what's going to happen up there above Ilen-dar. We've got to do some tall figuring and some swift scrapping before we're through."

"Sure." Tommy shrugged his shoulders. "There'll be a lot of

fireworks, I guess. But I wish I had a smoke just the same."

Ulana pouted. They spoke in English and she did not understand. But the expression of their faces forced a laugh to her lips, one of those silvery tinkles that caught at Blaine's heart strings. All that mattered now was to see her to safety — and happiness.

The cage slowed up and came to rest as the automatic control of its gravity energy functioned. The door rolled back and Blaine thrust his head through the opening, pistol in hand.

There on the floor of the corridor that led to the great dome room was a crumpled figure. Dantor! It couldn't be that they had slain him! Blaine was on his knees by the body, raising the blood-smeared head with gentle hands. A deep gash extended from over the right temple up into the scalp and the skull was crushed; a mortal wound. But the doughty heart of the aged scientist still beat on, weakly, but with determination. He opened his eyes and smiled.

"Ah, you have come at last," he sighed. "I have waited here to warn you and advise you."

"Easy now." Blaine straightened the helpless limbs and cradled the drooping head on his knees. Ulana was beside him, bravely holding back the sobs that were in her throat.

"I saw — in the crystal," Dantor whispered. "And Denari struck me down when I expressed relief at your escape. Carson — Ulana — Farley — you can escape if you do as I say. Antrid is doomed; the incorrectly proportioned charge burst the rocket-tube in several places and tore the muzzle asunder where it projected from the copper shell of our world. With the explosion at the muzzle a huge section of the copper casing was blown away and the atmosphere of Antrid is now escaping rapidly into the vacuum of space...."

Dantor closed his eyes, and a spasm of pain twisted his features.

Tommy expelled a shuddering breath, solemnly expressive.

The aged scientist fought off the grim spectre valiantly. He patted Ulana's hand as his weak voice resumed. "You will take care of her I know, Carson. Take her with you to your own world; make her happy." He fell silent once more.

"But how?" Blaine whispered.

"Oh yes, I am forgetting. The side passage — next one on the right — it leads to a storeroom of the oxygen helmets and

vacuum-tight suits in which you can step forth from the adjoining airlock. Your space ship is there ... unharmed.... In it you will be able to return ... and...."

But Dantor's spirit had fled the pain-racked body. Blaine closed his lids and stretched him on the hard metal floor, crossing the thin hands on his breast. Ulana sobbed openly for a moment and then bowed her head in silence.

"The last of the Rulans," Blaine said softly, looking down at all that was mortal of the Rulan scientist.

"No," Ulana whispered, "I am the last, my Carson."

"You'll become a good American, sweetheart," he said gently. "That is, if we get away from here." There was no time to be lost, at that. At any moment this Denari might find them. "Come," he begged, drawing her from the body, "we must hurry."

Following the passage indicated by Dantor they came at last to an open door. A noticeable draft blew outward and Blaine thought grimly of the scenes that were being enacted throughout all Antrid. The air that made life possible was escaping. And the news broadcasts from Ilen-dar would have notified the entire population by this time. There would be rioting, panics, murder and suicide in the cities of the accursed Llotta and in their subject countries. A frantic effort of the scientists to stop the gap would avail them nothing: it was an impossible task now. The construction of the great shell had been a different matter; there was some natural atmosphere remaining in those days. And, finally, they would suffocate, every last one of them. They'd die miserably, purple of face and with swollen tongues protruding.

The open door led to a railed-in balcony that looked out over the dome room. Machines still hummed there but the place was deserted save for a few scattered corpses: probably those of the Llotta who had objected when Denari usurped the throne.

A second door opened from the balcony into the store room of the moon-suits. At least these helmeted contraptions resembled the so-called moon-suits used by inhabitants of the inner planets when they visited a body having no atmosphere.

Ulana needed some assistance with the bulky equipment, and then Blaine climbed into another of the suits and locked his helmet. A moment later they were in the air-lock with Tommy, who had attired himself more quickly and was operating the

controls.

At the outer hatch they waited until the air pressure reduced to a practically complete vacuum. Their suits distended ludicrously now by the pressure within, they unclamped the hatch and stepped out to the surface of the great copper shell. It vibrated under their feet to the blast from the huge gap that was not five miles distant.

The RX8 was there as Dantor had said, a slim tapered, cylinder that gleamed, a thing of beauty, in the reflected light of Jupiter which now was millions of miles distant. The sun was not visible and the light of the mother planet cast long shadows on the copper plates. Pelting ice particles clattered resoundingly against the metal helmets: frozen moisture from the escaping air of Antrid.

Blaine cried out in surprise; then remembered his companions could not hear him. There were moving shadows over there, four of them, nearing the hull of the RX8. The Llotta had beat them to it. Denari, no doubt, intending to escape with a chosen few of his subjects. He broke into a run through the now blinding hail storm. He would have to head them off; else, Ulana was lost, they all were lost.

CHAPTER XII

The Last of Antrid

Tommy was running beside him now and Ulana was not far behind. They too had seen the danger. If they could not reach the vessel ahead of the Llotta; would not fight them off and gain possession, it was all off. They'd die here, horribly, on the roof of Antrid.

And the ray pistols were useless: they could not be fired inside the ballooning fabric of their suits without destroying it and themselves. There were only the hooks that were attached to the bulging sleeves — iron hooks for lifting — but these were heavy and sharp pointed. They might be of some use, at that.

Once they were completely blinded by a deluge of ice particles, Blaine could see neither the RX8 nor the waddling figures of the Llotta. He clung to his companions by means of the hooks, interlocking his with theirs, and waited for the storm to ease off. If ever it would! Pressing the thick glass window of his helmet against that of Ulana's, he saw that her eyes were wide with terror. But she smiled bravely and nodded encouragement. What a girl!

There was a momentary clearing a little way from the white wall and he saw the hull of the ship, a dim shape that loomed suddenly distinct and near. They dashed for the open port, still holding together.

One of the bulging, helmeted Llotta had reached the port and was scrambling inside. Blaine loosed himself and pounced on him, swinging one of his hooks in a sweeping, clawing arc. It caught in the fabric of the fellow's suit, ripping a foot-long slit. Like a punctured ballon it deflated and became a shriveled, clinging thing. The Llott hung there over the rim of the port, instantly suffocated and frozen stiff in the vacuum and intense cold of space as the air and heat of the suit was dissipated.

Blaine dragged the rigid body from the opening and flung it to the white powdered copper surface. Wheeling, he saw that another of the Llotta had engaged Tommy. Two of them: in fact, there were three swollen figures in that mix-up. And the fourth was advancing on a smaller figure that turned and ran. Ulana! In

a flash he was after them. Tom Farley would have to look out for himself, poor devil. With two of them against him, the outcome was dubious.

And then came a second snow-like deluge of white particles. He stumbled on, groping blindly; slipping, sliding in the precarious footing. It was ankle deep now, that powdery carpet of ice particles. Oh God, if that Llott devil got Ulana! He groaned aloud, a hideous mournful echo in the confines of the helmet. Groping, staggering there in the white silence, he gave up hope. The white-carpeted shell of Antrid heaved mightily from the force of some new concussion within, and threw Blaine scrambling.

Crawling now, feeling his way over the shuddering surface, he saw a dim huddled mass there in the pelting rain of ice. Moving, it was! Two bloated figures, one large and one small, rolling over and over: Ulana and the Llott who had chased her! He was there in one mad scramble and had dragged the fellow from her; was astride the rubbery inflated covering, clawing and tearing. The thing collapsed and went flat between his knees. He saw the mist of moisture-laden escaping air; felt the quick swelling and the jarring collapse as internal organs exploded from the atmospheric pressure inside the brute's body. Nauseated, he crawled away from the dead, grotesque-looking figure.

Ulana was on her knees, endeavoring to get to her feet. She had not been harmed, thanks to his good fortune in finding them. But where was the RX8? In the awful white silence, broken only by the eery patter of the ice particles on helmets and fabric, all sense of direction was lost. Through the double thickness of helmet lenses he looked into Ulana's eyes: for the last time, he thought.

And then the white shroud lifted once more. The ship was there, not a hundred yards distant! Tommy still battled one of the Llotta, desperately circling the wary, grotesquely bobbing figure and swinging those terrible slashing hooks. The other was down, almost covered with white. Out of the picture, that one, but the remaining Llott was giving his friend a tough time of it. With the girl clinging to him, their arms hooked fast, he scuttled over the treacherous, ice-powdered copper. He had to get there quickly, and help.

Tom Farley slipped and fell heavily. The Llott was on him in

a flash and they struggled madly there in splashings of white that hid them from view for a moment. Then one of them was up and the other lay still, a surprisingly shrunken and motionless figure.

The victor was coming at him then, bloated arms lashing out in swift, vicious circles. He had got Tommy, the damned swine! Blaine met his rush with a flying tackle that brought him down crashing. He lay still, the devil, knocked out probably by the metal helmet contacting with his skull. With arm poised for that slashing swing that would send him into eternity, Blaine peered through the lens of his helmet. His heart stopped beating and the upraised arm fell limp. This was no Llott: it was Tom Farley! Good Lord, he would have killed him in another second!

He tried to shake him; to bring him to. But he couldn't get hold of the bulging suit anywhere without danger of slashing it with one of those hooks. What if that fall had been fatal! Ulana was at his side now and he stared at her, white-faced, trembling in his uncertainty and horror.

And then Tommy opened his eyes. They saw him shake his head to clear it and then he, too, stared in horror. How close a call! Friend killing friend, out here in the air-less cold on the shivering shell of the dying alien world!

They helped him to his feet and through the entrance man-hole. His mind awhirl with emotion, Blaine saw that Ulana was inside and then followed as in a dream. He bolted the outer cover and turned the valve that would admit air to the lock. Soon they would be inside. With their protecting coverings discarded there would be the fresh air of the interior; light; warmth. Safety for Ulana. Away from the copper-clad world, they'd be on their way — home.

****

A little later, Blaine Carson sat at the controls of the RX8, Ulana at his side. Tommy was below, polishing and oiling and fondling his beloved machines. The surface of Antrid was visible through the viewing port, twenty miles beneath them and receding rapidly. Swinging in its new orbit, Antrid was gasping its last.

Over there, a few miles to the east, there spouted a column of white vapor that rose from a heaped up crater of ice which extended in a circle now many miles in diameter. Heavily laden with moisture as it was, the artificial atmosphere of Antrid pro-

vided a vast storm of frozen particles as it escaped into the absolute zero of space. For many days this would continue and the pressure within would drop gradually, down, down, until the air was so rare it would no longer sustain life. And there was no hope of repairing the break: the mountain of ice prevented getting at it from outside, and the rush of air from within made the handling of patch plates and brazing torches impossible. Besides, an area of supporting columns of more than a mile diameter had been wrecked by the blast of the rocket-tube. It would require an Earth year to make such a repair, even if they could retain that atmosphere. Antrid was done for, this time.

Abruptly, Blaine turned his head from the port and gave his attention to the controls. The RX8 pointed her nose upward, away from this terrible world of disaster and death — homeward bound. With a tremendous blast from the stern rocket-tubes she headed swiftly into the heavens. A thousand miles, five, ten, they shot into space with ever increasing acceleration.

And then a blazing orb was visible off to one side of the swiftly receding globe that was Antrid. Through the floor ports it shone, casting cheerful rays upward to the ceiling where they made a patchwork pattern of the gleaming metal.

"The sun," Ulana breathed, in awe. "I — I've never seen it, my Carson. It is most beautiful."

He drew her to him tenderly. "You'll see it every day, dear," he whispered, "when we're home."

Home — a wonderful thought! He'd not hoped to see it again; hadn't dared to since Antarro showed his hand back there in the asteroid belt. And now it was a reality. He was going home, and with him he was taking — Ulana.

"You — you think they will approve of me?" she was saying as he sent blasts from the steering rockets to swing them around on a new course sunward. "Your people, I mean. They will approve of your choice, my Carson?"

Anxiety showed in her wide-eyed gaze and she drew closer as if fearful of losing him.

If only she knew! If only he had words to tell her!

"Approve of you!" he said huskily. "Lord, girl, they'll love you! But not as I love you. It is the biggest thing — "

Tommy's discreet cough came from the head of the companionway. Blaine turned to glare savagely. His friend was standing

there, grinning like an idiot and extending a paper-wrapped package.

"Look," he exclaimed guilelessly: "cigarettes. I found them, a whole carton."

"Well, I'll be damned!" Blaine exploded, careful that he spoke in English. "All you think of, all you've talked about since we left the vessel, is your hankering for a cigarette. For God's sake, get out of here and go smoke yourself to death."

But Tommy was advancing, still grinning, still extending the package. "Come on, old kid, have one," he insisted. "It'll do you good; quiet your nerves."

And his friend dropped a tantalizing eyelid. In spite of his annoyance Blaine was forced to laugh. "Oh, all right," he said, reaching for the package of smokes; "I'll take one. Just to please you. But, beat it then, will you?"

Swaggering as he went and casting knowing glances over his shoulder, he was gone. Great little Irishman, Tommy: always smiling, always there in a pinch, never worried, he was the best friend a man could have. They'd catch hell when they got back, for losing a part of their precious cargo. Those miserly k-metal people wouldn't give them credit for salvaging nine-tenths of the stuff (luckily only about a tenth had been removed by the Llotta): they'd only cry about the amount that was lost. And Tom Farley would laugh it off: kid them out of it.

Ulana was smiling as if she understood. She *did* understand, God bless her. She saw into this wonderful friendship and was glad. It was great to have a friend like that — and a girl like this.

Hand in hand, they gazed into the heavens before them. To the girl it was a most marvelous sight, an omen of good fortune and of happiness to come. She nestled her head into the shoulder of the Earth man as she watched; spellbound.

For a long time the silence was broken only by the steady muffled purr of the stern rocket-tubes. The aroma of cigarette smoke drifted up the companionway.

Out there in the heavens was the sun, Mars, Earth, Venus; the dear old solar system was still intact, undisturbed excepting for the slight perturbation in the region of Jupiter. Blaine doubted if the influence was measurable insofar as changes in the motions of the inner planets were concerned.

He turned to the eyepiece of the telescope and swung the

instrument around to bear on the Earth. A cool green crescent was there in the field of vision: the eastern coast line of the Americas outlined clear and distinct.

"Look, dear," he whispered. "Home! Your new home is there; our home together."

She sighed happily as she gazed at the inviting sunlit outlines. "Home," she repeated, softly, reverently, "with you, oh my Carson — for all eternity."

FLIP THIS BOOK OVER FOR A SECOND GREAT READ!